Praise for *The Education of Margot Sanchez*

"Introducing Lilliam Rivera, one of the most unique and exciting new voices in YA. *The Education of Margot Sanchez* is funny, poignant, compelling, and authentic. She nails the music and conflict of an evolving Bronx, New York. I adore this novel."

—MATT DE LA PEÑA, Newbery Medal–winning author of *Last Stop on Market Street*

"In the hands of debut novelist Lilliam Rivera, Margot's choices—which friends? which boy? which future?—take on a tense urgency. Lively and telling, smart and compelling, Margot Sanchez is a character to take to your heart, and Rivera a voice to remember."

—KAREN JOY FOWLER, author of *The Jane Austen Book Club*

"*The Education of Margot Sanchez* shatters the myth of assimilation by exposing the loss and ache that comes with it. Instead, Lilliam Rivera tells the reader that there is nothing more powerful and beautiful than staying true to oneself."

—ISABEL QUINTERO, author of *Gabi: A Girl in Pieces*

"*The Education of Margot Sanchez* feels as classic as Judy Blume and at the same time entirely new. It's a rich, page-turning tale about a teenage girl stuck between a rock and the growing-up place."

—VERONICA CHAMBERS, author of *Mama's Girl* and *The Go-Between*

"With a passionate voice, Lilliam Rivera weaves a layered, complex story of a girl awakening to herself and her family."

—CECIL CASTELLUCCI, author of *Tin Star*

THE EDUCATION OF MARGOT SANCHEZ

LILLIAM RIVERA

SIMON & SCHUSTER BFYR

NEW YORK   LONDON   TORONTO   SYDNEY   NEW DELHI

SIMON & SCHUSTER BFYR

An imprint of Simon & Schuster Children's Publishing Division
1230 Avenue of the Americas, New York, New York 10020
This book is a work of fiction. Any references to historical events, real people,
or real places are used fictitiously. Other names, characters, places, and
events are products of the author's imagination, and any resemblance to actual events or
places or persons, living or dead, is entirely coincidental.
Text copyright © 2017 by Lilliam Rivera
Jacket illustration copyright © 2017 by Dana Svobodová a.k.a. Myokard
All rights reserved, including the right of reproduction in whole or in part in any form.
SIMON & SCHUSTER BFYR is a trademark of Simon & Schuster, Inc.
For information about special discounts for bulk purchases, please contact
Simon & Schuster Special Sales at 1-866-506-1949 or business@simonandschuster.com.
The Simon & Schuster Speakers Bureau can bring authors to your live event.
For more information or to book an event, contact the Simon & Schuster Speakers Bureau at
1-866-248-3049 or visit our website at www.simonspeakers.com.
Also available in a SIMON & SCHUSTER BFYR hardcover edition
Cover design by Lizzy Bromley
Interior design by Hilary Zarycky
The text for this book was set in Sabon.
Manufactured in the United States of America
First SIMON & SCHUSTER BFYR paperback edition March 2018
6 8 10 9 7
The Library of Congress has cataloged the hardcover edition as follows:
Names: Rivera, Lilliam, author.
Title: The education of Margot Sanchez / Lilliam Rivera.
Description: First Edition. | New York : Simon & Schuster Books for Young Readers,
[2017] | Summary: Margot Sanchez is paying off her debts by working in her family's
South Bronx grocery store, but she must make the right choices about her friends, her
family, and Moises, the good looking but outspoken boy from the neighborhood.
Identifiers: LCCN 2016008061 |
ISBN 9781481472111 (hardback) | ISBN 9781481472128 (pbk)
ISBN 9781481472135 (eBook)
Subjects: | CYAC: Hispanic Americans—Fiction. | Conduct of life—Fiction. | Love—
Fiction. | Family life—New York (State)—New York—Fiction. | Bronx (New York, N.Y.)—
Fiction. | BISAC: JUVENILE FICTION / Social Issues / General (see also headings under
Family). | JUVENILE FICTION / Love & Romance. | JUVENILE FICTION / Family /
General (see also headings under Social Issues).
Classification: LCC PZ7.1.R5765 Ed 2017 | DDC [Fic]—dc23
LC record available at https://lccn.loc.gov/2016008061

For Bella, Coco,
and David

CHAPTER 1

A cashierista with flaming orange-red hair invades my space the minute I step inside the supermarket. I search for Papi but he's walked ahead into his office already.

"Look who's here!" the cashierista announces while eating some sort of pastry. "La Princesa has arrived."

I wince as she calls me by my childhood nickname and not my real name, Margot. The rest of the cashier girls give my preppy floral outfit the once-over.

"What are you doing here?" She ignores the pastel de guayaba crumbs that fall on her too-tight shirt, which reads MIRA PERO NO TOQUES, a warning to the masses to look but not touch her looming chest.

Before I can even respond, Oscar, the manager, comes up to me and places a protective hand on my shoulder.

"She's helping us this summer," Oscar says. "Verdad, Princesa?"

"Well, more like supervising." I say this with just enough emphasis on the word "supervising" for the cashierista to shift her weight to her right hip. Oscar laughs at my work declaration/aspiration and offers me a pity pat on my shoulder.

I take a good look around. It's been a while since I've been here. Sanchez & Sons Supermarket used to be bright and cheerful, a welcoming oasis in a sea of concrete buildings. Now the blue paint is peeling, the posters are the same from five years ago, and there's some funky odor that I can't place. I spot a large sign with a banana dressed in a ridiculous mambo costume. The banana smiles back at me as if she's in on the joke. And she is. Everyone is. My year at Somerset Prep is being scrubbed away with every second I spend here and there's nothing I can do about it.

"This is Melody and Annabel. Say hello, girls." Oscar's gained weight since I saw him last, at my parents' annual Three Kings Day party. To combat his thinning hair, he keeps his head completely shaved. A Latino Mr. Clean. "Here's Rosa, Brianne, and Taina . . ."

These girls are just a couple of years older than me but some of the other women have been working at my father's supermarket for a while. Some even have kids my age. The ones with kids are a little bit friendlier but there's no point in remembering their names. I have no intention of staying here.

"You look just like a Sanchez," one of the older cashieristas says. "La misma cara of your father."

"Thank you." I'm not sure if it's a compliment or if she's saying I look like a middle-aged man. The cashier girl from earlier continues to eyeball me. I locate the exits and make a mental list of the possible escape routes. There's not much else I can do.

"Buenos días, Señor Sanchez."

A stock boy wearing a Yankees baseball hat tilted to the side and droopy, extra-large pants that fall off his hips greets Papi. Finally, Papi makes an appearance.

I adjust my skirt and pull down my matching short-sleeved top. The blouse barely covers my big butt. I might be overdressed but my stylish clothes are my only armor against perverted stock boys like this one, who now leers at me. Even with the hat I can still make out his *Dragon Ball Z* spiked hair, gelled so hard that it looks like a shellacked crown. I stare him down until he looks away.

It's seven in the morning on a Monday. This is how I'm spending my first day of vacation. I blame my parents for this summer imprisonment.

I was this close to joining Serena and Camille on their vacation to the Hamptons. Two months of hanging with the only squad that matters by the beach. It took some serious scheming on my part to secure an invite from the girls, right down to me doing things I never thought I would. There was that time they dared me to make out with some nerd, Charles from English class. Serena and Camille were joking but I did it. When I pulled my lips away, Charles's large eyes registered confusion, and then he turned bright red. What was truly messed up was that Charles didn't miss a beat. He covered up the embarrassment by laughing along with Serena and Camille. There wasn't much separating me from him. We were both outsiders in that school. Both didn't know how to dress. Both surviving. Still, I ignored that awful pit of guilt growing in my stomach because taking that dare was worth it. There were other things I did—denied my natural curls by straightening out my hair, stole some expensive lipstick— anything to make Serena and Camille notice me.

My parents have no idea who I have to compete with at Somerset Prep. How far down I was in the social caste system until Serena and Camille took pity on me. If I was going to be the great brown hope for my family by attending this super-expensive high school, I knew I needed to make friends with the right girls. Papi said to me on my first day of school: "Don't waste your time with idiots. Always look for the kids who stand out." Camille and Serena stood out because they were popular, like straight-out-of-a-CW-TV-show-episode popular. Fashion girls. I thought I was stylish but I had no concept of what that meant, with my dated vintage dresses in too-loud tacky colors. I tried to explain this to my parents but they called off my summer plans to teach me a lesson. Now I'm stuck in their supermarket in the South Bronx, far away from the sun and the gorgeous Nick Greene. Grounded. Stuck personified.

"Take a seat," Papi says. Chairs are arranged in a haphazard circle right behind the rows of cashiers. He points to an empty chair. "We are going to start the monthly staff meeting in a minute."

I pull him to the side, away from the workers.

"I made an appearance." My voice trembles a bit for a more dramatic effect. "Let's forget about this whole thing. I learned my lesson."

"Not another word. Siéntate. Let's get started, everyone." The cashieristas gather around him. If only Papi had sent me to work at the other Sanchez & Sons supermarket. The Kingsbridge store is way smaller and managed by my uncle Hector, who is a total pushover. Papi works at this location, which makes ditching that much harder.

"A couple of things. Oscar, I want a new display stand to promote July Fourth, not that old one." Papi leans against a conveyor belt. His sleeves are rolled up and his unbuttoned shirt flashes a small gold cross on a chain. He has hair that's more salt than pepper and a gut that spills a bit over his dress slacks. His name is Victor but everyone here calls him Señor Sanchez.

"People want to buy beer so set it up next to the seasonal items." He continues with the announcements while I compose another emotional plea in my head. How will I get out of this?

"Girls, make sure to push the customers to the display stands," Papi says. "Remind them of the holiday."

Stomping heels bang against the floor. The sound grows louder and louder. I join the others as they crane their necks to see what's up.

"Where's the coffee?" Jasmine, the only cashierista I sort of know, refuses to take her sunglasses off and greets everyone with a curled lip. "I'm not doing shit until I have some."

"You're late. Again," Papi says. "Sit down."

"Why didn't you tell me she was coming in?" she says. Although Jasmine's clearly pissed off at something I did or didn't do, she still comes over to me and plants a kiss hello with such force that I almost fall off the chair.

Jasmine has worked here forever. She even lied about her age to get the job. With her heavily painted face and a body that rules in these parts—big ass and even bigger tits—she looks way older than twenty. Her long, pointy nails are painted in Puerto Rican flag colors, reminders of the recent parade.

"You all know my daughter Princesa. She's joining the Sanchez family this summer to help at the store," Papi says. "Stand up and say hello."

I thought being born into the family made me a true

Sanchez. I face the cashieristas. A bored cashierista snaps her gum while her friend whispers in her ear. Someone laughs. There's no way to deflect the player-hating killer rays being thrown my way.

"You can call me Margot," I say. "My name is Margot."

No one is really listening to me, not even my father, who has turned his attention to the butcher.

"Who is going to train her?" Jasmine puts the question to the cashieristas. "Don't look at me because I always get the dumb ones."

I glare at her and then back at Papi but he is too deep in his conversation about meats.

"No seas dramática. You barely trained me," says the cashierista, who has managed to find another pastry to eat. "If anything, I had to show you what to do."

Jasmine looks like she's about to clobber the girl. The stock guys in the back seem too eager to witness some girl-on-girl action.

"I don't need to be trained." I say this loudly so that everyone is clear on what I'm willing to do. "I'm going to help Papi in the office."

"No, that's not what you're doing." Papi squashes my dream. "Jasmine, have Princesa start with the boxes in the back."

I'm not unloading boxes, not in these clothes and not with the pervy stock boys.

"Seriously, I'm better equipped by a desk," I say. "I can just answer the phones—"

"This isn't up for debate. Jasmine, show her what to do."

This is not happening. He never said anything about hard labor. Granted, I'm being punished but I thought this was for show. Papi didn't even want me to work at the supermarket. He was more than willing to ship me off to the Kingsbridge store but Mami put a stop on that. She wanted to make sure Papi kept an eye on me. I don't understand why I can't learn a lesson in the comfort of an office.

"These boxes don't belong here." A familiar voice rings out. The focus shifts away from my dilemma. "Get over here now!"

Although the sign at the front of the grocery store reads SANCHEZ & SONS, there's only one boy in this family. Junior, my older brother, walks in.

"Oh, look who it is," he says. "The Private School Thief."

My own blood shouts me out in front of everyone but I won't take this quietly. I'm not the only bad seed in this family.

"Yeah, well, at least I didn't get kicked out of college."

"I work for a living," Junior explains to the cashieristas. "I'm not trying to pretend I'm someone else. You know what she did? She charged six hundred dollars on Papi's credit card. So what if she's only fifteen years old? I would have called the cops."

Cashieristas suck their teeth in disapproval. Junior

is jealous because Papi decided to send me to Somerset. Junior's proven what a poor investment he is after he lost his wrestling scholarship. While he works I study at one of New York's prestigious prep schools. Basically, I'm the last saving grace for the Sanchez family. There's some unwritten family commandment that states that I will graduate from Somerset, attend an Ivy League school, and major in some moneymaking profession. The pressure is on to excel. They don't call me Princesa for nothing. I'm being groomed for bigger and better things.

Papi lets out a long sigh. "Go to your stations." His whole demeanor has changed. It's as if the control he demonstrated moments ago while running the meeting diminished the second Junior appeared. Junior is technically the assistant manager and I bet he loves to fling that title around like it means something. At home, Papi always reprimands Junior for something he forgot to do at work or for showing up late. No wonder this place is falling apart if Papi has to oversee my brother's messes.

I watch Junior approach each of the cashieristas with a lingering hug. They coo back at him in Spanish as if he's some telenovela star. Another reason why we don't get along: He's allowed to chat up every girl he comes in contact with while, according to Mami, I can't even speak to a guy on the phone until I finish high school. Not that any guy calls, but Nick might have if I'd had my way.

"Wake up, Princesa! I don't have all day to babysit you." Jasmine snaps her fingers at me.

"Please don't do that," I say. "I'm not some dog."

"You mean this?" She snaps her fingers again. And again. "Princesa, if that's going to bother you then you're not going to last here. Why are you working anyway? Don't you go to some fancy school and shit?"

"It's a mistake," I say. "This whole thing is a mistake."

"A mistake?" she says. "I don't believe in mistakes. There are only actions. It seems to me like you got busted big-time."

Her cackle hurts my head.

"No, that's not true."

"You didn't get busted for stealing?"

"I did get busted but I wouldn't consider it stealing," I say. "It was an advancement."

"Girl, please." Jasmine's eyebrows are raised so high that they practically rest on top of her head. "Who are you trying to play? You can't hustle a hustler. Let's go."

She pulls out a pack of cigarettes from her purse and leads me toward the back.

Jasmine doesn't know a thing about Somerset Prep. If she were in my shoes, she would have done the same thing. We walk past my brother, who's talking to a girl.

"Damn, your brother es un sucio."

"You don't have to tell me he's dirty," I say. "The guy only has one thing on his mind."

"He talks a good game but he's the type of guy that probably lasts for only five minutes. Then you're lucky if he doesn't make you cook afterwards."

I don't want to hear about Junior or anyone else's bedroom skills. It's gross and also I'm a virgin but it's not from lack of trying. The boys at Somerset are very selective. Although I've shed my cheap tacky style, I still don't get any play. I arrived at Somerset sporting a full-on tribute to girl groups from the sixties—pencil skirt, heavy black eyeliner, and slightly teased hair. In junior high, everyone thought I looked cute in my vintage outfits. Sometimes I would rock seventies bell-bottoms or try a version of a forties pinup girl. It was my idea to create an Instagram account, WEARABLE ART, to document outfits but the looks never translated at Somerset. Somerset boys just don't go for curvy girls in low-quality clothes. I ditched the pencil skirts that accentuated my full backside and followed Serena and Camille's tame, chic style. Taylor Swift is their icon and now she's mine too.

I follow Jasmine to the end of aisle four. The *Dragon Ball Z* boy sits crouched down in front of a tower of large boxes.

"Dominic, let her do it. I need to take a drag before they open the doors." Dominic grins as if he won the lottery.

"We need to restock this," he says. "You know, the female feminine things, the shampoos, and this stuff right here."

He points to an empty condom stand. My face burns red.

"Yeah, this is kind of important. Safe sex and shit." Dominic licks his lips and reveals a chipped tooth. "You know what I'm talking about, right? They probably teach you that in your cushy school. No glove, no love. We got all kinds of sizes up in here. Magnum, triple magnum, and for the girls who want . . ."

I close my eyes. I want him to shut up but he goes on, enjoying every humiliating second.

"After that, I got some other things for you to unload," he says. "Good luck, Princesa."

This can't be my life right now. I grab my phone to text Serena and Camille but there's no reception. Another cashierista walks by and laughs. Papi is delusional if he thinks I'll stay locked up in this depressing grocery world. The minute I find an out, I'm taking it. I roll my eyes at her before throwing a condom box meant for the display rack onto the floor.

"Ouch!"

The tip of my new gel manicure gets caught on a hard corner of the carton and tears. A tiny drop of blood emerges from the finger. Jesus. I need to connect with reality, my reality. I press down on the injury and walk away from the aisle, leaving the opened boxes a mess on the floor.

CHAPTER 2

Outside I check my phone and ignore the text from Elizabeth. Elizabeth and I used to be real tight. We did everything as a team, attended the same schools, sleepovers. But when her parents couldn't afford to send her to Somerset we drifted apart. The plan was always to go together. We stared at the Somerset website for hours and imagined ourselves perfectly posed in front of the school just like the students in their photo gallery. Elizabeth and I tried our best. We even applied for a scholarship for her but it wasn't enough. When she dropped the bomb that her parents wouldn't be sending her I freaked out. I wasn't supposed to do Somerset on my own. Now she attends an artsy public school called High School of Art and Design. Elizabeth doesn't understand the recent modifications to my style or why I no longer do the things we liked to do. She's kind of hung up on the past.

Instead, I call Serena.

"What are you guys doing?" I ask as soon as Serena answers the phone.

"Hello?" Her voice sounds muffled.

"It's me. It's Margot." It dawns on me that not everyone is expected to be at work by seven on a beautiful summer day.

"What time is it?" Serena says. "Why are you calling so early? I can barely hear you."

Serena and I sat next to each other in science class. I noticed her right away because she has blemish-free skin and straight dark brown, envy-worthy hair. We were paired up for a class project and that's how I found out she lived in this amazing brownstone in Brooklyn. Serena speaks three languages fluently so I asked her to teach me French and Taiwanese curse words. I spent most of my class time figuring out ways to insult people in Taiwanese, anything to prove I had a personality. She eventually invited me to sit with her and Camille during lunch but first she gently hinted that the dense eyeliner covering my eyes made me look like a raccoon so I stopped wearing it that way.

"I'm uptown and just wanted to check in," I say. "See what's going on."

"What?" she says. "Your voice keeps cutting off."

There's too much static. I pace up and down to try and find the best reception but the supermarket is situated right across from a park. The tiny bit of nature in the form of big green trees blocks my connection.

"What are you guys up to?" I ask again.

"I can't hear you and it's too early to be screaming into a phone," Serena says. "Call me later, please."

Click.

"Hello? Hello?"

Stranded at the supermarket.

"You'll find a better phone connection if you stand on the other side of the store."

I turn to the voice. I hadn't noticed him before. He wears a snug red T-shirt that shows off his lean baller's body, jeans, and a messenger bag across his broad chest. He pulls books from his bag and arranges them on a collapsible table. He's about my age, I think, maybe older. He doesn't look familiar. Not that I know anyone from this block but he's not dressed like Dominic or the rest of the stock boys inside. For starters, none of those boys would be caught dead wearing a beaded necklace.

"Thanks," I say. He nods and goes back to arranging books and pamphlets on the table.

I glance over to the supermarket. No one seems to have noticed that I've left, which is fine by me. The boxes can wait. I might as well find out why this guy is set up in front of the store. I stroll over to his table while he talks to a young mother. A grainy image on a brochure shows a neglected building with the words SAY NO TO THE ROYAL ORION underneath.

"They're displacing these families, forcing them out by cutting off their heat and hot water," he says. "These are our neighbors, mothers with young kids unable to get their basic needs met."

He directs her to a clipboard that holds only a couple of signatures. I grab a book with a black-and-white image of a woman and the title *Song of the Simple Truth*.

"I just need your name and number or e-mail," he says to her. Then he turns to me. "Sorry, but those books aren't free."

"Don't worry, I wasn't going to steal it." I place the thick book back where I found it. He needs to relax. I walk over to the other side of the table and read one of his brochures but it's hard to concentrate when I'm trying to listen to what he's saying. The mother leaves after she signs the petition. The guy finally directs his attention to me and points his pen to the image on the pamphlet.

"Have you heard what's going on right here on your block?" he says.

"I don't live here so I guess the answer is no."

"You don't have to live here to know when something is wrong," he says. "The Carrillo Estates owners are forcing their tenants on Eagle Avenue to vacate their apartments in order to build a luxury high-rise."

His lips are as dark as he is and full. His eyes are deep

brown. His beaded necklace goes perfectly with his whole boho-hippie style. He sure sounds serious.

"My name is Moises Tirado, and I'm from the South Bronx Family Mission." He sticks his hand out for me to shake. This whole formal introduction so takes me by surprise that I almost forget what to do. It's kind of cute. I like that. Yeah, he's kind of cute too. "I'm collecting names to present them to the community board. Would you like to participate in change?"

I look down at the other three signatures. There's a whole lot of white space up on that paper. I will not be the fourth person on there.

"No. I don't think so. I need to hear more to make an informed decision."

He rubs his chin and holds his gaze on me.

"I didn't catch your name," he says. "You're not from around here, are you?"

"My name is Margot and no, I said that already. I live up in Riverdale."

"Well, Margot. Can I call you Margot? Even people in Riverdale should be aware of the injustices happening here." He points again to the brochure. "What goes down here can easily go down in Riverdale."

"I don't lend out my signature so freely unless I do research first. You could be making this whole thing up."

I check for any traces of ink. Not that I have a preference

but certain tattoos can be a turnoff, like some chauvinistic writing done with a picture of a naked girl. A guy without any tattoos says something too. Like, maybe he's a good boy. From what I can tell, there are no tattoos but he does have some sort of scar around his neck. I try not to stare. I don't want to be rude.

"I only speak the truth. You can ask me anything you want. Anything." He says this with a slight smile. "I'll squash your doubts, Margot. Any hesitation, I will magically dispel."

Everyone here calls me Princesa. It feels good to hear my real name even when said by a stranger.

"Hit me with your questions. I'm ready," he says. "No, wait. Let me warm up."

Moises hops up and down like a boxer in a ring waiting for the bell to announce the start of a fight. He shakes his shoulders and rolls his neck. His performance is so ridiculous. It's hard not to laugh.

"Seriously? I'm not trying to a pick a fight," I say. "I just want the facts."

He stops and looks intensely at me. My hand automatically touches my charm necklace, the one Mami gave me last Christmas. I wish I would stop fidgeting.

"You're Junior's baby sister, am I right?"

My smile drops. He knows my brother. I'm not sure if that's a good thing. I wonder what else he knows about me.

Not enough. For starters, the way he addresses me is wrong.

"I'm not a baby," I say.

"No. You're definitely not a baby."

His expression is straight but there's a hint of something behind those eyes. Why do I feel so flustered? His face scrunches up as if he's studying my ancestral line, dating me back to when my great-great-great-grandfather lived in Puerto Rico wearing only a nagua right before the Spaniards got to him.

"I can definitely see the resemblance," Moises says. "You're way better-looking. No doubt."

"We don't look alike," I say. "Anyway, I work here. Well, actually, I started today. I'm helping out in the store, sort of like consulting. A marketing consultant."

His serious expression makes me speak more gibberish. He probably isn't buying my consulting line. The same thing happened with Serena and Camille. I was never one to lie but when Serena asked me what my father did for a living I couldn't admit that he owned two sad-looking supermarkets in the Bronx. I needed to boost the truth. Instead I told her my family owned a chain of grocery stores upstate. Serena and Camille didn't even bat an eye over my lie so I knew I'd made the right choice. The chances of them ever finding out the truth are so slim, it's worth the social currency.

"I was going to spend the summer in the Hamptons but I've decided to work," I say. "It looks better for college, although I still have time for that, but it's never too early. Working here is basically like a crash course in Marketing Strategies 101. It was either this or interning at Ketchum or IMG but going grassroots stands out more on those college applications. Do you know what I mean?"

The words flow as my tale becomes more elaborate. There's an adrenaline rush that comes with lying. It's the same feeling I get when the girls dare me to do stuff. Being bad. It's not really me but this other girl, a more exciting version of myself. If I stop talking Moises might actually see who I am. Besides, I can't tell whether he's interested or not. He listens, for sure, but his solemn demeanor only increases my word explosion.

"I'm planning on creating some social media campaigns. Work on their circulars. Take it to the next level."

Sanchez & Sons on social media? Circulars? I don't even know what I'm talking about. There's no way I can continue on this dumb path without sounding like a complete moron. Moises must see right through my bullshit demeanor. I stop.

"Anyway . . . I should head back."

"Wait. Don't leave. Give me five minutes to explain what I'm doing out here," he says. "I know you don't want to go back to work. You can use me as an excuse not to return. Besides, this is way more important than chilling on a beach or consulting for some supermarket."

For a second there that sexy smile of his got me rethinking my objections. It must be easy to follow Moises. Who wouldn't want to drop everything and sign his petition when social justice and a side of seduction are being served?

But he's no Nick Greene. After ignoring me most of the school year, Nick finally gave me some love. Tiny love, but love nonetheless. On one of the last days of school, I was caught up watching him walk in front of me when he abruptly stopped. I tripped, unable to navigate the high heels Camille insists I wear. Anyone else would have ignored me there on the floor, struggling to get up, but not Nick. He took my hand, helped me up, and asked if I was all right. Then he said my name. Margot. Serena thinks I have a good chance with him. He's smart but not a brainiac and he comes from money but not too much money so he's approachable. I could see my parents giving their approval. Not that Mami would ever allow me to go out on a real date with him but my relationship with Nick could exist at Somerset and on the phone. There are plenty of couples who communicate via texts. Nick would never have to know about Sanchez & Sons.

"You ever been to the Hamptons?" I ask. "I'm not talking about a one-day trip. I'm talking about staying at a beach house, like, living there?"

I notice the scar around Moises's neck again, a small rigid pink patch of skin. I try hard not to stare at it but I do.

"It's the life. You have no idea," I say. "You should think before you judge."

"Trust me when I say that those people lounging off others in the Hamptons are living with blinders on. The Eagle Avenue families are in fear of being kicked out of their homes." He pauses. "Can I ask you a personal question? How old are you?"

"I'm not going to tell you my age."

"There's no disrespect. Just trying to figure out where you land in the Sanchez family. I know Junior is older but I always thought his sister was way younger. But you're . . ."

"I'm what?"

He nods as if he's approved a thought in his head.

"Naw. Nothing. Just that I would have remembered you if I had met you before. I definitely would have."

He locks eyes with me. If I keep vigorously twirling my necklace I'm going to choke. I overhear my brother yell out orders to someone. This conversation is heading I don't know where but I better stop. I turn away.

"Hey, wait a second." Moises grabs my hand and presses a brochure into it. "Give me a chance. Let me explain what we're working on. Once you hear the stories about how badly these families are struggling you'll want to help."

For a few seconds our hands touch but I pull away and walk back to the supermarket.

CHAPTER 3

Two stock boys with mischievous grins greet me by the door. One shakes his head.

"You better not let your papi see you talking to some guy," he says.

I turn to the accuser.

"I was investigating what he was doing in front of the supermarket," I say. "Besides, my father and I don't have any secrets so what you're implying holds no bearing."

The stock boy looks confused. I flip my approach.

"Jerk!"

They laugh uproariously.

I've barely been here a full day and I've already been accused of being ignorant of the world's injustices and of exhibiting whore-ish tendencies. I jam the brochure into my purse and walk back in.

"So what did Moises have to say?" Jasmine asks. "Is he trying to sell you something?"

She thumps a can of salsa de tomate over and over against the price scanner with no result. Each time she creates a slight dent in the can. Exasperated, she presses the intercom and yells out for help.

"He didn't say much," I say. "Who is he?"

"Who, him? He's nobody. His brother is Orlando from up in the Patterson Projects. He's just some títere."

I peer back at Moises. His hair is curly and shorn tight to the sides. He has a bit of a growth, not a true beard but more like a goatee.

"He looks normal to me."

Jasmine smacks her lips with disgust. "He used to sell drugs like his bullshit of a brother. After Orlando got busted, I heard Moises ended up in Youth Academy."

I've never met anyone who was sent to Youth Academy Boot Camp before. The local news once did an undercover investigative piece on the brutal way kids were treated there. They even got an award for the coverage.

"Oh. That's terrible," I say.

"Terrible? Terrible is when you don't have enough to eat. Terrible is when you don't have enough money to take the train," Jasmine says. "What happened to him is pathetic. That makes him weak. Now he goes around the neighborhood trying to sound important, collecting signatures for I don't know what, but he's still a bullshitter just like his brother."

"How can you say that? You are so mean."

Jasmine motions to an elderly woman who's about to unload her cart on the conveyor belt to move to another register.

"I'm just being real. Real talk," she says. "Don't be mad because I speak the truth."

"Does he still go to Youth Academy?"

"What the hell do I know?" she says. "I'm not social services."

Jasmine grabs the microphone and yells for Junior. I open a pack of M&M's and toss a bunch of them in my mouth. This talk about boot camps and drug dealers freaks me out. Sugar will comfort me.

"You need to pay for that." Jasmine holds her hand out. "That costs a dollar."

"Are you serious?" She can't be. My father owns this place. I should be allowed to take whatever I want. I'm practically an owner. She doesn't budge. I pull out a dollar in change and slam it on the conveyer belt. Why does Jasmine have to bite my head off?

After a few more minutes, Junior comes down. He looks pissed. Another day, another argument with Papi. He should be used to it by now. Papi's been riding him ever since he lost his wrestling scholarship. First, Junior couldn't keep up with the other wrestlers. He kept complaining that the coach didn't understand him, that it was too hard. There were heated discussions on the phone, with Papi imploring Junior to shape up. After he busted his knee during a match, the coach dropped Junior from the team. No more scholarship. Junior didn't even try to keep his grades up. He just sort of gave up and stopped attending classes. Academic probation soon followed. Within weeks of that Papi made the decision to pull Junior from the school.

Now Junior works as assistant manager but everyone knows that Oscar is really Papi's second-in-command. Junior is twenty-three but his face is haggard, drawn in with bags under his eyes. Before, he cared only about wrestling. Working out. Healthy food. Tight shirts that showed off his cut arms. Now he smokes too much. Drinks too much. Does everything too much. Worse than all of that, he wears Ed Hardy bedazzled-dragon shirts.

"You're going to have to be nice to me for me to fix this." He flirts with Jasmine. My brother never turns it off.

"How about 'fuck you.' Does that work for you?" Jasmine says this in the sweetest of tones. Her cold expression is pretty funny.

"You didn't say that last night," he jokes. Gross.

"Ay, pobrecito, you wish we were together last night," she says. "You will never, and I repeat, never handle this body. You can beg or pray to la Virgen María. It ain't ever going down. Anyway, I'm not going to say anything more out of respect for your sister."

"Wait a minute. Aren't you supposed to be somewhere?" Junior says. "Those boxes aren't going to unload themselves."

I cram the rest of the M&M's into my mouth.

"I have an injury." I show him my chipped nail. "Besides, I don't think a minor should be handling prophylactics."

"Isn't that Orlando's brother?" Junior notices Moises. "What the hell is he doing out there?"

"He's collecting names for some meeting," I say.

Junior contorts his face as if he got a whiff of a dead rat.

"What the fuck. Naw. That's not gonna work. He needs to take that somewhere else."

"What are you talking about?" I say. "He's not doing anything bad."

Moises has every right to set up on the sidewalk. It's not like he's selling something illegal, just a bunch of books. Talking to people as they walk in and out of our store isn't a crime as far as I know.

"He's disturbing customers," Junior says. "That's what he's doing."

"No, he's not."

People find this exchange amusing. Even Jasmine chuckles. But not Junior. He walks away but I refuse to let this go. He needs to listen to me. Who made him King of the Bronx?

He points to José and Ray, two of the stockiest rough-necks on the Sanchez team, and says, "Come with me." I follow Junior and his henchmen outside. They stand in front of Moises's table. Moises welcomes the new audience by raising his voice and continuing his talk.

"They create insulting campaigns like SoBro or Piano District and try columbusing our neighborhood. But this is the South Bronx and we take care of our people," he says. "Together, we can stop Carrillo Estates from continuing their assault on hardworking families."

Junior grabs a couple of the brochures, acts as if he's reading them, and then throws them back on the table. The move is so very dramatic and stupid, like some bad reality TV reunion episode.

"You need to take this out of here," he says. "You're blocking the entrance to the store."

"Sorry, I can't do that." Moises rearranges the pamphlets. "This is a public sidewalk."

The henchmen wait, itching for the green light to make their move. A crowd of about ten starts to circle around us, mostly guys from the nearby car repair shop and customers from the supermarket. This isn't good. *El Show del Mediodía* is about to start, starring my jerk-off brother versus the innocent yet somewhat arrogant Moises.

"I don't think you heard me," Junior says. "I'm giving you five minutes to take this down."

Moises puffs his chest out in defiance. He turns to a man who's wearing a green T-shirt with PUERTORIKAN written in a poorly drawn imitation of a Heineken beer bottle and begins his speech.

"Have you heard what's going on on Eagle Avenue?" He hands the man a brochure. "Families are being harassed on a constant basis. You remember how it went down in the seventies, when corrupt landlords started burning down buildings to get rid of their tenants. It's about to go down again."

"Ha!" I can't help it. To see someone ignore Junior's self-proclaimed rule is a rare treat. This is pure comedy. I love every second of it.

"Can you believe this guy?" Junior asks the henchmen. The henchmen don't answer. They keep their mean face on.

There's a sudden change in the atmosphere, an intense sensation of incoming violence. I can't keep quiet and wait for the impending destruction to arrive. Someone has to take a stand.

"He's right," I say. "This is a public spot. You can't legally stop him."

Moises sneaks me a playful grin. My stomach does a flip but I stay in control. There's no need for him to think I'm on his side. I'm just stating the truth.

"This has nothing to do with you," Junior says. "Go back inside."

This is the first time I've ever seen my brother rage in public. I should show Junior respect. He's older. It's what I've been taught to do. But he's out of order.

"No," I say. "This affects the supermarket and I'm part of the company. You need to listen to me."

"Roughly seventy-five percent of the tenants live under Section Eight. The other twenty-five percent are elderly living on a fixed income. They are your loyal customers and you are turning your backs on them," Moises says. Someone in the crowd eggs him on with a "Preach."

"Get your facts straight. We know who lives in that rundown building. Addicts and pros," Junior says. "Why aren't you telling them about how Carrillo plans to relocate the good-paying tenants while the condo is being built? They can move right back when it's finished."

"They say they want to show good faith but as soon as that building goes up," Moises says, "only ten apartments will be allocated for low-income families out of eighty-three units."

Moises's hands lie flat against the table as if he commands a group of soldiers about to head out on combat. He's captured the attention of the crowd. No one can deny those numbers. Even I can see that it's unfair. Junior looks desperate.

"He's playing you, son," one of the henchmen tells Junior. "There's no respect."

Enraged, Junior walks right up to Moises. Inches away from his face. He mutters under his breath, loud enough for only Moises to hear. Moises meets my brother's glare.

"You're being a jerk!" I cry. "Stop!"

The henchmen block my way. They create a huge protective wall of muscle and funky body odor.

"Vete adentro, Princesa." One of them implores me to go back inside.

"This isn't right!" I yell. "Stop acting like you're in charge."

It's no use. I'm a tiny speck of nothing in a sea of masculine crap. There is one person who can stop this power move. I run in, past Jasmine gossiping with a customer and an old lady asking a stock boy to help her carry her bags out to her car.

My father sits hunched over some accounting books. He's conversing with Oscar in a serious voice.

"I can't talk right now. I'm in the middle of—"

"Papi, you gotta stop Junior. He's beating up on that guy outside with the table." The words clumsily stumble out of my mouth. "I mean, he's about to beat that boy outside. C'mon!"

I expect no less than a running brigade to the rescue, of Papi storming out, with me by his side, ready to put Junior back in his place.

Papi looks wearily at Oscar and then back at me. He rises from his chair and stares across to the commotion. Junior pushes Moises and there's a scuffle between them.

The henchmen pull Junior away but in the process they kick the table over. Moises's books and pamphlets scatter across the sidewalk. The henchmen's construction boots tear into pages.

"They're going to kill him!" I yell, tugging at Papi's arm.

"No," he says. "This doesn't concern you. Esto es asunto de hombres."

This is men's business? He can't be serious.

"I can't believe you're saying that." I try hard to control my shaky voice.

"Let your brother do his job," he says.

"I didn't know his job included harassing innocent people."

"This is what I mentioned on the ride to work this morning. Life is not as neat as you're used to, especially here. Let us do what's best and don't worry about it."

And just like that, Papi goes back to his numbers.

I stand there with the hope that he'll change his mind but even Oscar looks away. I can't believe it. This is how things are done here. What a joke. I hate everything about this place. I slam the door behind me.

Junior and his goons stroll back in. The henchmen console Junior as if he were the victim. Moises kneels on the sidewalk. His books destroyed. He slowly picks up the remainder of his belongings and leaves.

For the rest of the day, I unload boxes and send distress

messages to Serena. She finally texts me from the beach. I'm so jealous I eat two packets of M&M's.

Don't be down, Serena writes. Do whatever you can to get over here. I heard Nick comes next week. Remember your goal.

Nick throws a blowout bash in the Hamptons right before Labor Day. After feeling sorry for me, Mami said she would let me have one summer reprieve. But August seems so far away.

The only good thing that's come out of this is that I now have the perfect excuse to never return. My parents thought I could learn about responsibility. Guess what? My innocent, delicate mind has been scarred for life with street violence.

I pull out my notebook and start a list:

THINGS/PEOPLE I HATE
Mami, for destroying my social life
Papi, for allowing Junior to become a Neanderthal
Junior, for becoming a Neanderthal
This supermarket
Everyone else.

Papi wants me to be a silent partner in Sanchez & Sons Supermarket, so be it. But as soon as we get home I will open my mouth and let Mami know that their glorious summer idea has backfired big-time.

CHAPTER 4

Although Riverdale is technically in the Bronx I don't like to think of it that way. The Bronx is the Bronx. Riverdale is different. There are more houses and parks. It's not as crowded and it's clean.

Our simple Colonial-wannabe home gets a rating of five out of ten, ten being a megamansion. It's not a run-down shack or anything like that. There's just nothing particularly extravagant or exciting about it. Farther down our street real houses exist—large mansions with many rooms and long front yards. But at least we live next to the rich. We live Rich Adjacent.

Papi pulls into our Rich Adjacent driveway. I continue the silent treatment.

Instead of going to my room, I head straight to the bathroom located off the side of the living room. Mami keeps this room filled with white flowers. She read somewhere that white has a calming effect on people. She also likes to keep self-help books on display for easy access and rotates them with what's currently popular. This month, the book *Getting To It* sits nestled next to Rita Moreno's memoir. Decorations are done via the latest issue of *Interior Design* but it's always at a lower price. I know this because I've been to Camille and Serena's homes and they do not have white flowers or cheap prints of Monet hanging on the walls of their bathrooms or living rooms. They have real art by real people I've never heard of.

I still wear the same face I kept the whole time Papi drove us home. Rage Face. I wipe off the remainder of my lipstick and switch up my look with the sad image I want to present to Mami: a girl who's been traumatized. I've seen way too much. A girl who should spend the summer recouping on the beach.

"Dinner's ready!" Mami yells. She wears a bright pink blouse, designer jeans, and teetering-high heels. We look nothing alike except for the almond shape of our eyes.

Papi carries spreadsheets with him. He arranges the pile on the dining room table. While Mami serves baked ziti, extra crispy on the sides, Papi smiles feebly at me as if showing teeth will make me forget what happened only a few hours ago. I take my seat across from him. The seat next to mine is meant for Junior but he almost never shows up for dinner. Junior is supposed to stay at the store until closing time but I bet he just uses that as an excuse to avoid family hour.

I sit and wait for my cue.

"How was your first day?" Mami asks.

Hello cue.

"It was fine until Junior almost killed a boy," I blurt out before I dig into the food.

No need to explain more. Mami lives for this. When she found out that Junior got kicked off the wrestling team, she clutched her chest as if she were about to have a heart attack. It wasn't the fact that my brother lost out on a major opportunity or that he was injured. She freaked out over what the neighbors would think once they found out. "What will we say to them?" she asked. There's a constant fear that our family embarrassments will leak out to the masses. Thankfully, I was accepted to Somerset Prep so my good news offset Junior's downfall.

"Por Dios, what is going on over there?" She taps the edge of her plate with her polished nails. Her latest diamond ring glistens.

"Carmen, you're working yourself up for nothing," Papi says. "It was just a bum out causing problems."

Unbelievable. Papi's rewritten history, but has he forgotten that I was a witness to the whole thing?

"He wasn't a bum! Why are you lying?" I say. "He was

just a boy. He wasn't doing anything wrong and Junior went all lethal on him and you did nothing to—"

Papi slams his fist on the table. I jump. He closes his eyes for a few seconds and inhales deeply.

"I already went over this with you. You're old enough to understand and since your mami wants you to learn some life lessons this summer, here's lesson number one: Let us handle the trash outside. You should be thanking your brother for protecting the store."

Mami shakes her head. Her blond highlights emphasize her brown skin. Something I hadn't noticed before: Mami is a silent partner just like me. When I was young she would dress me up in the cutest getups and bring me to work with her. This was when she helped Papi manage the supermarket. I had my own little shopping cart and although the shelves were too high, most of the customers would lift me up so I could reach for a bag of cookies or some candy. They proclaimed my adorableness and my parents beamed at me like I was the winning toddler in a child pageant.

But that was long ago. Now Mami prefers to stay home and take useless courses at the local I've-Got-Too-Much-Time-on-My-Hands School. She folds and unfolds her napkin.

"Look." I thrust my trembling hands at her. "I was so freaked out. I tried to stop the madness but no one listened to me. I'm too scared to go back there. I can't. I just can't."

37

There's no doubt, the drama I'm laying on is thick. Junior isn't here to correct my version of the events. This is my only chance.

"I don't know, Victor. Maybe we should reconsider," Mami says. "Margot could stay home and help me around the house."

Pump your brakes. It's my turn to shake my head vigorously. This is not what I want. There's still time for me to go to the Hamptons. I don't get her. Has she forgotten how we bonded over Somerset? She caught me in my room in complete misery over how I wasn't connecting with my classmates. Unlike Papi, who thinks everyone will instantly fall in love with me, Mami understood that feeling of being an outcast. She told me about those rough first months in New York, recently arrived from the island. She sat beside me on my bed and gently caressed my forehead. Time finds its way of working things out, she said. Later, when I told them about Camille's invitation to stay with her at her parents' beach house, it was Mami who convinced Papi to let me go. Soon after, she began searching for beach houses to rent herself. The Hamptons is our baby unicorn and it's slowly galloping away.

"No. I want her to learn that there is a price to pay for her actions. It's what we should have done with Junior," Papi says. Papi blames Mami for my brother's academic failure. Somehow his flunking out of school was her fault.

I'm not sure how that works, something about how she always babies him.

"Can't I at least look for another job?" I say. "I don't like the way the stock boys stare at me."

"This is your first job. You will have to learn how to navigate different types of personalities. It's the same as in school," Papi says. "Not everyone is going to understand you. Have patience. You will figure it out."

Mami clucks her tongue like a chicken. "If she's going to work at that supermarket, you need to pay attention to her instead of running around doing who knows what." Her lips curl a bit.

"You mean working," he says. "It's been a while since you've had a job. Perhaps you need to come back to the supermarket to be reminded of that."

"Be honest, Victor, you don't want me there."

Oh my god. They're turning my serious social problem into an excuse for marital argument number 500.

"Can you please focus? I want to vote on working somewhere else, somewhere safe, like the mall. Let me work at Traffic."

Traffic is an ultracool boutique with expensive designer clothes and, I'm sure, a hefty employee discount. The store is located at the Cross Country mall in Yonkers so I would never run into anyone from Somerset. And if that were to even happen at least I would look fashionably fly.

"I guess you didn't read what happened in the mall," Papi says. "Bunch of kids fighting in the Game Spot."

This battle is being lost but I still go forward.

"I don't understand why Junior didn't talk to the guy," I say. "He wasn't doing anything, just collecting signatures. We are living in America, or does the South Bronx have separate laws?"

"This boy may have good intentions but he's a little misguided."

Papi explains how the building Moises was talking about is a known drug house. Many people have overdosed there. Prostitutes frequent it.

"The owners have been trying to clean the place up for years. Putting condos in that area helps us," he adds. "There'll be better-paying customers and that's good for business."

"Sure, but . . ." My tactic fizzles fast. There's got to be some angle I can take. I offer up the only thing I have left.

"Using force shouldn't be the only alternative. What Junior did was terrible."

"The neighborhood is a little rough. It's not a life you're used to but you'll learn to love it," Papi says. "Also, this is nonnegotiable. You have to pay back the six hundred dollars you stole plus an additional two thousand dollars to help with back-to-school expenses. You've got ten weeks."

"What? I thought I was just working off the six hundred dollars. You didn't say anything about back-to-school stuff," I say. "You're not even paying me a living wage! I'm only getting seven dollars an hour. I don't even think that's legal."

"You are going to pay the twenty-six hundred dollars, no matter what, even if that means having to work weekends. Start doing the calculations." He taps his fork on the side of the plate.

I feel like crying. I give Mami a pleading look but she sits there and says nothing.

"I'll talk to Junior," Papi says. "Your brother is a bit of a hothead but he has the store's safety in mind. You understand that, don't you?"

Papi reaches across the table. His large hand, rough but warm, engulfs mine. There are tiny wrinkles around his eyes. He has the weathered face of a man who spent his childhood under the strong Puerto Rican sun. He tugs at my hand again to make sure I caught everything he says. I read him loud and clear.

"You're good with the Facebook, Insta—yo no sé," he says. "Maybe you can figure out how to place the supermarket on there. What do you think?"

"Great," I mumble. Besides stocking condoms I will now be the social media serf.

"Princesa, whether you like it or not, you're spending the summer with me." He lets go, grabs his fork, and points it at Mami. "Just be happy you're not spending it with her."

She gives him a dirty look.

"Que cómico! Very funny," she says, and serves him another huge heap of baked ziti.

"I can still go to the summer party, right?" This time I ask Mami because she understands how important the party is to me. It's the only thing I have to look forward to. I pray they don't take that little bit of fun from me.

"Bueno, it depends." Mami looks over to Papi. She wants to say yes but she can't give me permission. Papi has the ultimate say.

"If she does her job, then maybe she can go to the party," he says. "Maybe. Me entiendes?"

I'm stuck for ten weeks and there's no guarantee that I'll even be allowed to go to Nick's party. It's not right. I will have to figure out a way. I'm going to Nick's even if I have to spend every hour shelving crap.

Mami serves us carbonated water from a new machine she ordered online, explaining in tedious detail how the machine works and why her brand is better than the brand used by the neighbors.

Papi and I act as if we're listening to her.

My phone vibrates. Serena sends me a pic of Camille by the pool. She's sipping what looks like a frozen coffee drink. The text reads: U r missing out. Serena follows it with another picture of two guys hoisting Camille up in the air, ready to drop her in the water. Her mouth is frozen mid-scream; her legs are sprawled out.

I text back with questions: Who r those guys? Where r u? When was this taken? Serena responds with, Don't you wish you were here!?! I stare at the picture of Camille about to be thrown in the water and relish that seconds later she was a soaking-wet heap. I beg Serena to send me the "after" picture. It's my only reprieve to hate on Camille when clearly they're both having a blast without me.

They r Camille's cousins. They're kinda hot. Right? Serena texts.

They're okay. Moises is better-looking but I don't text Serena that. She doesn't need to know what went down. No matter how much I pretty up the supermarket incident I'll still end up sounding tragic. Instead, I give her a line of how wonderful my first day at work went.

Aren't you trying to get out of it? she responds.

Most definitely. I will join you guys soon enough.

I add a few happy faces to the text. I don't want Serena and Camille to feel sorry for me. They've done that before, like when I mispronounced some long SAT word or when I made the mistake of saying I wanted to join the fashion club at school. "You don't really want to do that, do you?" is what Camille said, her face confused. I told them I was only kidding. Serena and Camille aren't fans of clubs.

There's a knock at the door. Mami answers it and

seconds later Elizabeth walks into the dining room. I should be happy to see her. I should. It's not like we had a blowout or anything but the truth is I still hold a tiny bit of a grudge from when she abandoned me at Somerset. Our friendship is not as intense as it used to be, especially when she made friends so quickly at her school and I was left flailing like a fish.

"Dizzy Lizzy!" Papi teases. "How's the family?"

Elizabeth giggles although the joke is so played out. She dyed her hair blue, which doesn't look right on her. Her clothes don't make sense either. There are colors clashing with prints. Each fights for wardrobe domination. Nothing matches. Art school has changed her style just like Somerset changed mine.

"Family's good," she says to Papi. Then to me: "Why haven't you responded to my text? I thought you had a supermarket accident." She leans over and peers at my phone. "Oh, you responded to those friends."

How funny. On my first day at Somerset Elizabeth didn't answer any of my texts. There's nothing worse than sitting by yourself in a cafeteria while everyone around you is paired up. The only thing I could do was send long, one-sided messages to Elizabeth so that I wouldn't look like a complete loser. When we spoke later she was so excited about her cool new friends that she barely mentioned the messages I'd sent her.

"Sorry, no time," I say. "Training."

I put my phone away. Elizabeth has never met Serena and Camille. Whenever I mention them, she can't hide her disapproval. She never says anything vicious, she's not like that, but there are little things. A face. A raised eyebrow. When I told her I wanted to spend the summer in the Hamptons, she wasn't happy. Elizabeth thought we would explore the city together. She wanted me to meet her new friends. You would love them, she said. I was too focused on reaching the Hamptons.

She accepts a plate of food from Mami and sits in Junior's empty seat.

"We should hang out one day after work. There are a lot of things happening in the city. I mean, if Mr. Sanchez will give you a break from price-checking oranges."

Elizabeth is interning at an art museum this summer. Ever since third grade, she's always been into art. She's talented too.

"I don't know," I say. "I'm unloading boxes and according to him I'm on lockdown."

"You can't always be stuck there," she says. "C'mon, you owe me."

She will never let me forget. Elizabeth and I have a pact to watch every single Tom Braverman action movie on opening night, no matter how bad it is, and they are usually pretty bad. We've had huge crushes on him since we could have crushes on guys. That was our thing. Eat popcorn. Love Braverman. Last month, I broke the pact by seeing Braverman's latest with Serena and Camille. Elizabeth was so upset.

"What's up with this?" I change the subject and tug at a blue strand.

"There's a painting in the museum that has this exact same color. I knew I had to rock it. People at work love it." She shrugs. "You could stand to use some color in your hair."

Never. Camille and Serena are about highlights. And the hair has to be flat-ironed straight. I wake up every morning to deny my curls with a blowout. Anything else and I'll stand out. Elizabeth is on some other trip and I can respect that. It's just not what I'm doing.

"Remember that time when you decided we needed bangs and I ended up looking insane?" She snorts, which makes her laugh more.

"Yeah, that was not cute."

It was my idea. My love for girl groups was just beginning and I insisted we needed bangs and a tease-out. I cut Elizabeth's hair but didn't realize her bangs would curl up. She trusted me, which was probably her first mistake. I insisted on documenting it on our Instagram account, WEARABLE ART. Back then, I wasn't afraid to look and act weird.

"So funny," Elizabeth says.

I always used to take the lead and Elizabeth always went along with me. The blue hair is daring but not in a way that makes sense. What benefits does it have? I'm daring because it will get me somewhere. Now that I'm in with the right crowd at school I have to keep up. Blue hair will work with the artsy-fartsy crowd at the museum but not at Somerset.

Elizabeth stays until she finishes her meal. When she leaves I text Serena to check in with her and Camille.

CHAPTER 5

Sweat trails down the back of my neck to the crevice of my butt. I look down and notice the deformed wheel on the shopping cart I've been fighting with for the past five minutes. It's the end of week number one. Instead of having me do any kind of social media for the supermarket, Papi decided I first needed to herd carts out in the parking lot. I crave shelving instead of this tiny new hell. Cars honk at me to move out of the way. One woman complained how dirty the carts were and how I should use a disinfectant to wipe each of them down. "You don't want to start an Ebola crisis, do you?" she asked. No, I do not want to start a deadly disease but I also don't want to do this.

I stop in the middle of the lot, pull out a hair band, and put my once-sleek do up in a lopsided bun. This is the worst, and this ugly uniform jacket adds nothing to my situation.

Before I faint Oscar thankfully comes out with a gallon of water.

"Sit down and take a break!" he yells. I join him underneath the store's awning. "How's it going?"

"I think I'm going to die," I say. "It's too hot to be out here."

"Did you know that these carts cost more than a hundred dollars each? It's true," Oscar says. "What you are doing is so important. It might seem trivial but it's not."

A hundred dollars! Maybe I should bill Papi for each cart I collect. He can deduct it from the twenty-six hundred I owe.

"We should upgrade to the automatic-lock carts but they cost too much," Oscar says. He pulls a towel from his back pocket and wipes the perspiration accumulating on his bald head. "Sometimes it's good to do work with your hands." He pours me a large glass of water and I gulp it. "It's humbling work. You are almost done."

He shows me his rough hands and we compare. My poor chipped nails. So not cute.

A young white woman exits the store. She pushes a cart with groceries. There's a college student vibe coming from her. Maybe she's attending Fordham University. Still, it's pretty far to be shopping over here if she's going to that school. The woman leaves the shopping cart by me.

"This neighborhood is changing," Oscar says. "They

can't afford the city rents anymore. The Bronx is cheaper."

"That's good," I say. "Right?"

"Sure. You would think. But you have to prepare for that change," he says. "It's good that you are here. Maybe you can help your father figure that out."

How can I possibly help? I'm in high school. I bet people at Somerset never have to deal with this kind of pressure. Papi does that to me all the time. Any dream I may have about my future is dictated by my family's hopes. The burden falls on me to lift up the Sanchez family but how can I do that? I've never worked a day in my life until now.

"I can't even figure out how to align these carts together," I say. "Besides, the store is doing well. It's always busy."

"Oh yeah. We're doing okay but they are building a new supermarket right by the other Sanchez location," he says. "New buildings everywhere. Have you noticed?"

Maybe Moises is right. New condos mean new supermarkets. Better ones. I've never thought of that before. Overheard Papi telling Junior to expect more visits to the Kingsbridge location, something about making sure that things are running smoothly. I guess Papi is worried about the new construction too. We stare at the college student as she walks toward the bus stop.

I don't say this to Oscar but I don't want the responsibility. What do I know about hundred-dollar carts and this neighborhood? I just got here. I drink the rest of the water and go back to my cart-rescue mission. When I'm done, I take a detour to the break room to cool off.

"You don't know anything about anything," Jasmine is saying to a cashierista. They're supposed to be by their stations but I guess they're on their break. I make myself an iced coffee and sit at the far end of the communal table.

"Ese pendejo fucks everything that breathes," Jasmine continues. "If you let him chat you up once, he'll pull out his little wiener in five seconds flat. Trust."

The cashierista dabs her wet eyes with a crumpled tissue. Even before his name is mentioned, I know who they're talking about. Junior. This is probably how this poor cashierista's love life played out: Junior showed her some interest, personally "trained" her, then got bored and moved on to his next victim. From the looks of her, she fell hard.

"I don't want to talk with *her* here," the cashierista says. She angrily dries her tears. I feel sorry for her for falling so quick on someone so not worth it. But I have my own problems to worry about. I won't apologize on behalf of my brother.

It's nasty how much of a pig Junior is when it comes to the cashieristas. The other day two of them started arguing over their work schedule, accusing him of playing favorites. Papi had to put his foot down on that. One girl even tried to sidle up to me with lunch invites, trying to extract information from me like what my brother does on the weekends and with whom. I tried not to answer with specifics especially since I don't know or want to know. Being his baby sister holds some weird power over them. They think I will magically crown them his new girlfriend.

"You don't have to worry about Princesa," Jasmine says. "I bet she doesn't even know half the shit her brother does here. Am I right?"

That's not entirely true. The more time I spend here the more Junior's work life is revealed, and it's not pretty. How he yells at the stock boys. How he tries to override Oscar's ideas. How he's a sucio to the girls. There's another thing too. He's kind of sloppy. Wrinkled shirts and all. What is he doing during those long weekends? When he comes home—if he comes home—he smells of smoke and alcohol. Mami continues to do his laundry and never mentions it. He's a guy, old enough to do what he wants. I don't have that luxury.

"I don't trust her," the crying cashierista says as she gets up. Her chair scrapes the once-white linoleum floor and leaves a long dark mark.

Jasmine shrugs, opens a compact mirror, and applies black eyeliner. Her tongue sits on the corner of her open mouth like an anchor to hold her head steady.

"Why doesn't she, um, tell my father what's going on with Junior?" I ask. He basically sexually harasses this girl, or girls, and no one does a thing about it. They accept his deviant behavior simply because he's the boss's son. It's not right.

Jasmine applies blush that covers her cheekbones with a shimmering streak of pink. She doesn't respond.

"Well, then," I say. "Maybe I'll tell Papi."

Jasmine slowly places her compact down.

"If you say one word to your father I'll kick your ass," she says. "She's got a kid at home from her ex. She lives with her mom. She needs this job. Don't fuck it up for her. In a week, she'll be over Junior and his tiny dick."

With one cheek glittery pink and the other bare, Jasmine looks like a demented clown. I stare at my shoes because who wants to be threatened right before lunch? I can say whatever I want but what the hell do I know? This isn't my world. The rules of engagement are unknown to me here. It's as if I'm reliving that first day at Somerset when I walked around like a huge question mark unable to navigate other people's intentions. Junior high was so easy. The school was near home so everyone knew each other. So what if Elizabeth and I were into shopping for vintage clothes and dressing up in retro looks? I never felt weird because Elizabeth was by my side.

"Sit down," Jasmine says. She lets out a sigh. This time she's less ominous, more inviting. "Come. Sit by me."

I take my time and scoot over to where she is but I don't sit right next to her. Can't be sure when she'll turn on me again.

"Can you sing?" she asks after a long pause. I shake my head. "Too bad. I need a backup singer for my demo. I'm making a demo. Dance music. You didn't know I could sing? I can and I write songs too.

"This." She flings her arms with exaggeration. "This shit right here is only temporary. You're not the only one with moves."

I didn't know I had moves. We both work in some run-down supermarket. Any money I make goes straight to Papi. So, no, I wouldn't say I was making moves.

"There's this guy I met a couple of months back. Big Bobby G," she continues. "He's a legit producer and he's going to produce my single. Watch. I'm going to blow up. Not everyone has to go to some fancy school to hit it big-time."

Does she know how many singers truly make it out there? I won't burst her bubble. But who knows, maybe she'll be a Boricua Beyoncé.

"What do you want to do?" she asks, and I'm taken aback by the question. What do I want to do? Finish high school, of course. Get into the best Ivy League school out there. Unfortunately, my grades aren't that amazing. I'm smart but there are others who are way smarter. Papi believes Somerset guarantees acceptance into any university but the competition is fierce.

"I don't know," I answer. "I like social media stuff. Maybe marketing."

"Like Facebook and shit?" she asks.

"No. I mean like a publicist. Never mind."

When Elizabeth's parents converted their guest house into an art studio for her, she named it the Creative Collective. So official. Elizabeth believed we would somehow work together. I would be her manager/publicist, getting the word out to prestigious art galleries. I even made a list of galleries in New York and figured out how to write a press release. Elizabeth said Somerset would help our cause. I could make some cool connections.

"You want to be a professional liar" is what Junior said when I told him about my silly marketing dreams. I have to aim higher. Lawyer. Doctor. Something that earns a seal of approval from Papi and Mami. A publicist? Camille's mom hires publicists all the time. I might as well say I want to be a secretary, not that there's anything wrong with that, but different goals have been placed in my life. My parents need a daughter with a job they can boast to people about.

"You have to find what you love and do it," Jasmine says. "Get it right, get it tight. Because these mocosos out here aren't going to help you. You got to help yourself. You know what I'm saying?"

At least Jasmine pursues her dream. When I tried to show initiative, I got shipped off to the supermarket. Papi and Mami are certain I'll prove to everyone that the Sanchez stock is worth every penny they've spent on Somerset.

Graduation means instant scholarship to a university. Yeah, right. Even if I do end up at a good school, what if I turn out like Junior and flunk out? What if it's in my blood to sabotage my life? He can't get his shit together no matter what type of guidance Papi gives him. His latest scheme is to convince Papi to invest in some bar in the Bronx. It's sad how many times he's been shut down.

Then there's me. Struggling to maintain good grades. Trying to look like the others. Sound like them. So that I won't be "that girl." I'll just be one of the girls. What matters is keeping the Sanchez dream alive. It might not be my vision of my life but it's still a decent dream to have. It benefits everyone if I succeed.

"If you want to talk to your papi about anything, you should tell him to stock up on some gourmet coffee instead of this wack Bustelo," Jasmine says. "I'm just saying."

"Yeah, sure," I say. "I'll talk to him."

Dominic unloads the boxes while I stack the products in a typical pyramid. I work on a promotional stand for some new products: piña colada mixers, ready-made for lazy summer drinkers. It sounds nasty.

For reasons unknown, I'm always paired with Dominic. And although I pretty much can't stand his guts, I've been able to hold down my anger to the level that I don't curse him out every single time he opens his mouth. Dominic enjoys getting a rise out of me. Since that's his MO, I try my best to ignore him but there are times when I can't even do that. His pants hang so low that I can see his underwear. He catches me staring.

"What do you know about piña coladas, Princesa?" he asks. "We should do a little taste test. What do you think? You and me, out in the back. I promise I won't tell your pops. C'mon."

Dominic has a girlfriend. I don't take him seriously. Since I don't pay attention to his dumb remarks, he reverts to reciting a rap song I've never heard before.

The pyramid starts to shape up. Before stacking the last can, I take a good look at the ingredients listed in the drink. The contents are unpronounceable, with tons of sugar. Why can't we sell organic juices? That would draw in the college students.

There's a community garden nearby that has a great selection of vegetables and fruits. We should figure out a way to buy our fruits from them. I don't think Papi ever noticed the garden until I pointed it out to him on our drive in the other day. Papi should stop displaying pyramids of crap and start figuring out ways to amp up his grocery game.

Junior walks over. We haven't said much to each other since his run-in with Moises. Every day I scan for Moises's table. It's an automatic thing. I figured he would show up. Prove my brother wrong. I guess not.

"Good job," Junior says. For once I get some love.

The tension in my shoulders relaxes. Maybe Papi will release me from my duty once he sees what an exceptional stock girl I've become. Every day I make sure to accomplish one minor thing, something that doesn't involve too much hard work but has maximum advantage. Yesterday, I friended the scanning gun and priced the canned vegetables. Canned peas. Canned carrots. When Oscar saw my completed work he sang my praises up to Papi. Papi gave me a hug. Before he walked away I asked him about the Hamptons but he just smiled. Oh well, I tried.

"Tomorrow, I want you to help at the deli," Junior says.

Sandwiches. Meats. Stinky cheese? The deli is one of the busiest departments. No. Please, no.

"When am I going to be a cashier?" I say. "I can do simple math. I mean, how hard can it be to scan an item and punch some numbers?"

"Go over to Roberto before you leave today so he can give you more details."

"Who?" I ask.

"You still don't know anyone's name." Junior smacks the top of his head. He lowers his voice. "Princesa, try to make an effort. It's not that hard."

Try. Like he tries to endear himself to the girls here. Is that what he means? I may not know people's names but at least I'm not trying to screw them.

"What's up with you and that cashierista, the one with long black hair?" I ask. Jasmine didn't say anything about talking to Junior.

Dominic chuckles behind me. Junior's face falls. His eyes are red. The shirt he has on is the same one from yesterday. How rough was his night that he couldn't even change his clothes?

"She was crying about you."

"Shut up and go to Roberto," he says, and hands me an envelope. "And here."

"What's this?"

He walks away. I catch the glance he gives in the direction of cashier row. It probably wasn't the right move to say something to Junior. Whatever. He should be aware that there are consequences for his lecherous actions.

Although my money goes right to Papi, I'm being blessed with a pay stub detailing the money I make but don't keep each week. There must be a mistake, the amount is so low. I should have made close to $500 for two weeks of work but this states I only made $447.70.

"Where is the rest of my money?"

"Uncle Sam," Dominic answers. "Taxes."

This blows. How is anyone able to buy nice things? Imagine if I had to pay bills, like my phone bill. Two weeks and I barely make enough to buy one cute dress.

"I'll miss you, Princesa," Dominic says. "Unloading

boxes won't be the same. Don't forget the hairnet."

Who said anything about a hairnet?

THREE THINGS I WOULD RATHER WEAR THAN A HAIRNET
Dominic's Yankees baseball cap
A pointy elf hat
A skull tattoo with the words "Save Me"

CHAPTER 6

Every time I try to direct the customers to pick a number from the ticket dispenser, they straight-up ignore me. I'm bombarded with deli orders at an insane pace in Spanish. I can speak Spanish, follow it, even read it but they speak way too fast. At Somerset, I was automatically enrolled in advanced Spanish only to have classmates correct my verb conjugations. There's no time to figure out if I have the right accent here. I'm too slow. And the more I try to keep up the more impatient the customers become.

"Por favor, repite su orden, señora?" I ask the abuelita to repeat her order. She scrunches her face. The wrinkles create an accordion of skin on her forehead.

"Donde está Roberto?" she yells. "Roberto!"

It's only been a day since I started work at the deli section with Roberto. Unlike Dominic, Roberto doesn't like to talk. He gives me side-eye for hours at a time until he's exasperated. Only then does he come out from behind his workstation to talk to the bothered ladies who continue to barrage me with questions I can't answer. They only want to talk to him, not to some strange girl in a tacky hairnet.

I pull on the plastic gloves. It's impossible to use my phone with them on, not that anyone is trying to contact me except for Elizabeth.

Hang out after work? Paloma and I are heading uptown, Elizabeth texts. There's a free concert at a park near you.

Elizabeth met Paloma on the first day of school. For the longest time Elizabeth's script was: "Paloma makes jewelry. Paloma is so talented. She is so funny." This isn't something I've admitted to Elizabeth but I'm jealous of some phantom girl I haven't even met yet. It wasn't long before Elizabeth sported a handmade necklace by Paloma. It's a simple piece of jewelry with the word GATA etched on a silver cat-shaped pendant. I don't know what it's like to create a piece of art with your own hands. Right now the only art I'm producing is slices of cheese.

I pull off one of the gloves and text her back that I can't go.

Elizabeth adds a bunch of silly faces and a funny video of her at the museum. Art. Art. Art. Then a severe close-up of her face, which makes me laugh. This, of course, pisses Roberto off.

At least you're looking at pretty things, I text back. Welcome to my world.

I sneak a video of Roberto giving me the side-eye, my large plastic gloves, and the underutilized ticket dispenser. The story of my summer in one ten-second clip. Elizabeth responds with more funny faces.

Haha. Doesn't look that bad, she texts. Gotta go.

A group of church ladies arrive and insist on speaking only to Roberto. Elizabeth is mistaken. This is the worst. I won't get anywhere if I let them scream at me.

"No Roberto today!" I yell. They stop. I announce that from now on we will use tickets.

"When I call out your number, you can tell me what you want," I say. "Number four!"

They are not happy. One cries out to the Virgen María to aid her in securing her morning deli meats but eventually the ladies give in. When I call out another number, they scan their tickets and act as if they've won the lottery. There is progress. Soon they help other customers by alerting them to the new deli process. It works! It feels good to finally have control even if it is just deli meats.

"Buenos días, señoritas!" Papi appears. "Have you met my daughter yet?"

"Señoritas!" The church ladies tease him. "It's so nice you allow your daughter to work with you."

Allow? Yeah, right. Papi grins widely. He loves having

me here. His Princesa. His baby doll. His prize pony.

"This is for now, but next summer, she'll work at a law firm," he says. "We need a lawyer to help me out of this business headache."

Now he's placing bets on me becoming a lawyer. Last month, it was on me going to medical school. Every time he makes these proclamations, I cringe at the pressure. But there's an opening in his statement so I take it.

"Don't you think he should let me have a little break before I start law school?" I ask the church ladies. "I should go to the beach. Have fun with my friends."

Papi's smile stays plastered on his face while a couple of the church ladies cluck their tongues. Spending time with your family is what Jesuscristo wants for his beloved daughters, one of the church ladies says.

Not Jesuscristo. I have no pull with this crowd.

"Es verdad," Papi says. "Besides, what would Roberto do if Princesa wasn't here to help?"

Roberto only offers a side-eye to the conversation and continues to slice up ham. And that's when I notice him out the window. Moises is back and he's setting up his table out front. This time he's come with reinforcements. A muscular man with a few menacing tats carries a box while another guy follows him. Backup or not, Moises has some sort of death wish. Why else would he come back here?

"Yo, Junior!" says Ray, one of Junior's henchmen. "El pendejo ese está afuera."

A slight smirk appears on Junior's face as he spots Moises. My palms begin to sweat underneath the plastic gloves. I look at Papi but he's tied up with the church ladies. Junior walks down to the floor and conspires with the henchmen. Things are going to turn ugly quick. Right when Junior is about to exit the supermarket, Papi calls his name.

"Did you fix that freezer back there?" Papi says. Ray and Junior look guilty. "Do it now."

"In a second," Junior says. "I got to take care of this first."

"No. It can't wait."

Junior curses while I let out a sigh of relief. The church ladies are all unaware of the drama that's unfolded right before them but a glance from Papi tells me he knows what's up. Papi excuses himself and walks back to his office. I have a tiny window to help free Moises from impending doom. I ask Roberto if I can go to the restroom, then take a detour outside.

Moises seems so unaware of his fragile life. He casually talks to a group of emaciated, disheveled men. The dull gaze the men have as they circle around him makes me feel a bit uncomfortable.

"Yeah, pana. I know what you mean," one man says, his face pockmarked. "They're always trying to bring us down, you know? Like me, man, they were trying to get me off the methadone, telling me I needed to follow the procedure. Shit."

Moises never diverts his attention although I can't see how he stays there. Even from where I stand I can smell the man's metallic stench. Moises doesn't let on that it bothers him. He concentrates on what the man says and acknowledges his pain in dealing with a bureaucratic health system. Someone in the group notices my slow crawl toward them.

"Wait, wait, I know you! Yeah, I know you. Your name is . . ." The homeless man claps his hands together with the hope that the thunderous sound will snap his memory back into shape. No such luck. Worried about the length of time he takes to figure out my name, I cut him a break and tell him.

"Naw, that ain't it. They call you Princesa." He gives his partner a high five. "I know I'm fucked up but I ain't that fucked up."

The men soon head over to the Drug Freedom Center and leave me with Moises.

"Good morning," Moises says. "You look different. I'm feeling your supermarket style. You are mercado ready."

Oh god. I forgot I'm still wearing the hairnet. Whatever. There's no time for a fashion do-over.

"Do you like getting into fights?" I say, exasperated. "That must be it. Why else would you come back here?"

Moises does that thing with his chin, rubs it and gives me that puzzled look.

"This is my neighborhood." He points to the housing projects down the street. "I grew up there and I live a few blocks down that way. Why should I be afraid to come here?"

"Well, I don't know, maybe because my brother wants you out?"

"I can't control the future," he says. "So I don't live my life in fear of it. Do you?"

What a strange thing to say. I spend my waking hours figuring out my future—what to wear, what to say, how to say it. There are scores of yellow pads with lists of things I plan to accomplish in any given day. A list makes me feel like I'm in control, even if it's just lines of things I hate. I carry a miniature pad to jot down everything.

"Do you know about the work being done at the Drug Freedom Center? Once a month they hold a family potluck slash jam session with live music. I host sometimes. Good music," he says. "So, I haven't seen you in a bit. Have you had a chance to think things through?"

"What?"

He grabs his clipboard and pen. "Say no to the Royal Orion."

This is what he wants. Moises is not interested in how I'm here to save his life. He wants my signature.

"Oh yeah, about that," I say. "There are two sides to each story so I can't rightly commit to either. I heard that most of the tenants stopped paying rent. And that there are a lot of drugs in that building. It's the reason why they're being evicted."

From his expression I can tell that what I'm saying isn't news to him.

"Hmmhm." He rubs his chin. "Maybe you've got a point there."

Is he teasing me? There's no way he is giving up that easily. He returns to his table, pulls out a stack of pamphlets, and distributes them to anyone who'll take them. Most people push his hand away.

"If you want to have a serious discussion, let me buy you lunch," he says. "I owe you."

I scan the area to make sure no one, not the church ladies or Junior, heard him. I can't figure Moises out. First he schools me on social causes. Next thing I know he wants to hang.

I shake my head.

"Why not? What are you afraid of? It's just lunch." He chuckles. "I won't make you give out pamphlets. Well, not until after lunch."

"I'm not afraid but I don't know you. You could be some crazy, whacked-out person. Besides, I didn't do anything."

My finger works overtime on my necklace.

"You stood up for me." He lowers his voice, all sexy and stuff. "I'm talking about sandwiches."

There's a part of me that wants to go but I won't. I

can imagine what Serena and Camille would say. No matter how good-looking or nice Moises is he's not elevated enough. Giving out pamphlets doesn't sound like much of a life goal. My goal is clear. This year, I will be seen with the right Somerset guy, someone worthy of my time. A future lawyer or doctor can't have lunch with some guy who collects signatures or hosts jam sessions.

"Princesa, inside."

Junior stands by the supermarket. He does his street strut over to the table. My heart races because I've been here before and Junior looks primed to start something. But I refuse to move.

"You can't set up right in front of my supermarket," Junior says.

Moises is about to respond but the muscular guy next to him presses his hand against his chest. The man extends his other hand.

"My name is Douglas and this is Freddie from the South Bronx Family Mission. On behalf of Moises and the Mission, I would like to apologize for any misunderstanding that might have occurred the other day."

Moises keeps his eyes on me, not on Junior, which causes me to blush. If there is an apology being made Moises refuses to be a part of it.

"There was no misunderstanding," Junior says. "Your worker was causing a fire hazard."

Junior acts as if he had a valid reason for his bruto actions. What went down the other day had nothing to do with blocked entrances and everything to do with macho pride BS.

A couple of people stand around in anticipation of another Junior freak-out. Junior can't afford to do that, not after what Papi told him about how this situation can escalate into people turning on us. Customers chose to buy from us, Papi said, but they can easily go somewhere else.

"We can set up our table right over there." The boy named Freddie points to a few steps away from the store. "We're not in anyone's way and people can still receive the lowdown on Carrillo Estates."

"Does that work for you?" Douglas asks. He offers his hand again to seal the deal. Junior pauses before accepting it.

"Make sure he knows what's up." Junior stares hard at Moises. "The minute he blocks the store is the minute I move him."

"You heard that?" Douglas asks.

"Yes," Moises says.

Junior can't stand him. There has to be more to their connection for him to be so pissed off at Moises. But what?

"Princesa!"

Papi stands by the entrance. I ignore him. Why does he have to come out at this moment? They're both trying to play me in front of Moises.

"Buenos días," Moises says.

"Don't clog our entryways," Papi responds in his mean voice.

"Of course." Moises hands out pamphlets with a smirk firmly planted on his face.

Papi puts an arm around me and leads me back inside.

"You seem to have way too much time on your hands." He hands me a mop and a bucket of water. "This is for you. Aisle one."

Before I can defend myself, a toddler runs across the supermarket completely covered in what looks like jelly. A large purple splotch awaits me.

I want to join the little boy and run screaming across the store too. Week number three sucks. I've made $660 but I can't even touch that money. Papi embarrassed me in front of Moises and there are roughly forty days until Nick's party. Practically a lifetime.

CHAPTER 7

oday I decided to venture out of the supermarket and cross the street to St. Mary's Park. I pass a string of little kids lined up to buy coquito. They yell out their orders as if the louder they are the quicker they can taste the iced coconut treats.

"Dame uno de cherry!"

"I want one de coco!"

Unfazed by the chaos, the vendor yells back while she adjusts the tiny umbrella that protects her from the sun.

"Un peso. Un dollar!"

I usually eat in the break room but Junior decided to pay the room a visit. The flirting and cooing back and forth between him and the cashieristas made me sick so I grabbed my lunch and snuck out the back. There's an empty bench far away from the kids. I sit and make a call.

Although I dialed Serena's number, Camille answers the phone and in the background I hear laughter. Nervousness takes over. There's no denying it. I'm missing out on good times and inside jokes that'll be shared when we return to school this September.

"Hey, it's Margot," Camille announces to the girls.

Of the two, Camille is the bitchier one. I've never met anyone so hypercritical of everything (except maybe my mom). Sometimes my Bronx accent comes out too strong. Or the color of my lipstick clashes with my outfit. Camille never hesitates in giving her opinion. There are no filters. Serena warned me that Camille was hard-core. I had no idea how hard.

Camille lives right in the city with her mom and stepdad in an apartment building that has a doorman. Her parents also own a beach house in the Hamptons and each year they go away on fancy European trips. She lives the most glamorous life. Designer clothes. A personal credit card. Everything I wish I could have. I tolerate her minor jabs at me because I want her life. Mami said to give Somerset time, while Papi's advice was to stick with the kids who stood out. Camille, with her long thin legs, looks like a model. Girls and guys want her. I'm following their advice. I'll win Camille over no matter what.

"Who's there?" I ask. My laugh is a little too loud.

"Just some of the girls." The receiver is covered. Are

they talking about me? If they saw me they would. My dress is wrinkled and my perfume has been replaced with eau de bologna. I tug my stray hairs into the bun as best I can while I hold the phone.

"Tell her Nick asked for her." The voice sounds like Serena but I can't be sure. I also can't tell if she's messing with me or if he really did ask.

"Are you guys serious?" I ask. "What did he say?"

More giggling. They don't get it. Guys at Somerset always talk to them but I've been the ugly stepsister of the group, the one that's barely noticed by guys or even girls for that matter.

"He asked why you weren't here." Serena grabs the phone away from Camille. "He looks good. Some other girl is going to hook up with him and you'll never have a chance. And he said—"

Someone there interrupts by singing loudly and out of tune.

"What did Nick say?" I beg. They keep singing.

From a distance, I see Moises walking toward me. Of all the benches in the park, he selects the one right next to mine. Why? This can't be happening.

"That was it. He didn't go on," Serena says. "Be happy he remembered your name. Progress."

I feel self-conscious. Should I move so that Moises doesn't listen to my conversation? Then again, why should I? He sat next to me. Screw that.

"What do you think I should do?" I ask. "Should I send Nick a text?"

"No!" Serena yells. "Get a grip, Margot."

"Yeah, you're right. Sorry."

There's no reason for the way I act. Total amateur. Serena and Camille sing again. I won't yell, not while Moises is listening to my every word like he's my parole officer. Instead, I hum along to their song.

"Oh my god, what are you doing?" Serena laughs and I think I hear a snicker from Moises. "I wish you were here! It's not the same. We are having so much fun. Come out."

There's a tightness in my chest. At least Serena misses me. That's something.

"I wish. I'm working on it. It's complicated."

"Tell them the Hamptons is a mandatory school trip," she says. "You'll be suspended if you don't go."

I got the idea of stealing Papi's credit card from Serena. She said her parents never seemed to mind when she borrowed their credit card. After I pulled the card from Papi's wallet, we met at Serena's nice brownstone in Brooklyn. Sitting on her bed while Camille figured out my summer attire, I was able to bury the crime deep down because I belonged. Camille loved being my stylist and I loved the attention she gave me. That day I was no longer the quirky sidekick with the annoying accent.

"If Nick doesn't work out, there's always Charles," I overhear Camille say. Charles is the geeky guy they dared me to kiss. It's a lame joke she always goes back to. Camille can be such a bitch.

"Stop playing around," I say. "Just say hi to Nick for me."

"I will," says Serena. "I'll give Charles your number too."

"Haha." I can't keep this up. They won't share any more Nick stories now that Camille has brought up Charles. I've been the butt of the joke before. Camille disses me and then Serena joins in.

"I'll check in with you guys later," I say, and hang up on their laughter.

I turn to Moises. "There are like five hundred benches available. Do you have to sit here?"

He scoots over and pulls out a small blue towel. He lays the towel out and pulls items from his messenger bag: a sandwich, a malta, and a bag of potato chips.

"This is my spot. I come here every day," he says. "I'm sure there's another bench where you can figure out the whole Nick dynamic in private."

"Seriously?" I say. He doesn't own this bench or this park. I pull out my salad and try not to take too big of a forkful. He, on the other hand, takes huge bites out of what looks like a Cuban sandwich.

After a long silence, he asks: "So, how's that working for you?"

"Excuse me?"

"Nick? How's your boy Nick treating you?"

Of course he paid attention. I revert to my current defense mechanism when I feel cornered—I lie.

"It's great. I mean he's great. He knows how to treat a girl right. Always buying me things. Jewelry. All kinds of stuff."

"That's what you like?" Moises sizes me up. "Living that baller life."

"Yes. It's nice. Not like the guys here. The idiots here probably just treat you to a White Castle hamburger and call it a day."

"Naw. We prefer McD's. It's classier," he says. "So, Nick. What's his background?"

He flashes a sly smile. No way will I talk about Nick and my nonexistent relationship with him, even with that grin. I can't stop staring at Moises's lips.

"Why are you in my business?" I ask.

"Just looking out for a sister."

"I already have a deranged brother. I don't need another one. Thank you."

"I don't mean to pry," Moises says. "Just curious. Somerset is an old school and they definitely lack diversity but you're there so that means something."

"I'm not the only Latina there." Another lie. The first day Papi dropped me off at school, he said with pride, "You won't find any títeres here. Only blanquitos, white people." Skin color matters to my parents. If you're a little dark-skinned, a trigueñito, that's bad luck. Lighter? You're definitely blessed. My brother Junior takes after my mom. They are both Afro-Latinos. I take after Papi.

"Cool," Moises says. "So how long've you been seeing him?"

Nick. Right. A vision pops up of Nick on the beach walking hand in hand with some other Somerset girl. They make perfect sense, like an Urban Outfitters catalogue spread.

"You're so nosy," I say. "Don't worry about it."

"Okay, okay. I'm just making conversation." Moises raises his hand in defeat. "I'll stop with the questions."

He goes back to his sandwich. I go back to my salad. This is awkward. I don't want to talk about Nick but I don't want to sit here in silence. It's silly.

"How do you know my brother?" I ask.

"He used to hang with Orlando, back in the day."

"The brother in jail?"

That was so rude. I can't even control my mouth. What is wrong with me?

"Sorry," I say. "Someone mentioned it to me the other day."

"You don't have to apologize. Everyone knows Orlando is in jail." A flicker of sadness appears on Moises's profile but only for a second. I don't remember my brother ever once mentioning Orlando. My parents would never have allowed him to have a drug dealer as a friend.

"The friction between me and Junior is nothing new," Moises says. "We got history."

"History," I say. "What kind of history?"

I knew something was up by the way Junior went ballistic on Moises. I wonder how deep their connection is.

"It's buried. I no longer run in the same circle as he does." He says this before taking a sip from his malta.

"What do you mean?" I ask. Junior usually hangs out with a trio of guys who live in this neighborhood. As far as I know, they mostly go out to bars and nightclubs. Big-headed guys in search of late-night action but none of that involves drugs. Does it?

"Junior and his boys are more interested in crushing than in causes. If I'm not collecting signatures I'm leading restorative justice workshops at the community center or voicing my opinion in some meeting," Moises says. "There's work to be done and I don't have time to waste searching for the club life."

Always so serious.

"Jesus, do you ever have fun?"

He cracks up.

"Sure. Most definitely," he says. "In fact, I can show you a good time."

I almost choke on my salad. "Oh my god! You can't be serious with that line!"

"I'm dead serious, Margot." His expression is poker-faced but there's a glimmer in those eyes. He is totally messing with me. "Helping your brothers and sisters is fun. It's the reason why back in the seventies people were down with the Young Lords Party, emphasis on the party. I bet you didn't know that tiny bit of Latino history."

This time, we both laugh. He is funny. I like seeing that side of him. But it doesn't last long enough.

"You should come with me one day so I can show you what's going on at the Eagle Avenue building where Carrillo Estates wants to build condos," he says. "There's Doña Petra. She's a widow who's lived in the building most of her life. The ceiling in her bathroom collapsed one day. She's been having to go next door to a neighbor's apartment because she's too afraid to take a shower."

"Oh," I say.

I do feel bad for the old lady but the run-down building I should be focused on is my father's supermarket so that I don't have to continue to live in shame. Or better yet, find a way for Papi to sell it.

"Don't get me wrong, there are people there who haven't paid rent in months," Moises adds. "But those are just a few. You can't judge a book. What happened in El Barrio is about to happen in the Bronx. The deadly G word."

"The G word?"

"Gentrification. High-rises built on the backs of those living here for years." He punctuates his words with his hands as if that will keep the anger from boiling over. "Carrillo Estates is the first of many. Who will stand for the Pet-

THE EDUCATION OF MARGOT SANCHEZ

ras of this neighborhood? It's on us to be their voice. We can't be silent. Now is the time. You feel me?"

I find myself caught up. It's kind of hot to see a guy be passionate about something. Nick sort of acts that way when it comes to soccer. He bounces a soccer ball endlessly through the hallways of the school. He wears those super-thick socks and tight shorts. But I don't think that's quite the same thing. I also remember what Papi told me the other night, how new condos bring new customers. Does that make me, us, a sellout?

"Yeah, we've got to add pressure. Let the community be aware," Moises says. "So, what's up? You got a man or are you holding out for your boy Nick?"

Whoa, back it up. He's so blunt and all over the place. It's hard to figure him out when he switches back and forth like that. I'm not prepared for what's happening right now, unless I count the recent list I wrote titled "Five Imaginary Conversations with Moises." (Number three: If Moises says, "I like it when you wear your hair naturally curly. Forget what the beauty industry is trying to sell you," your response should be: "I knew you would like it.") The list is obviously pure fiction.

"What's so funny?" he says. "I guess I should say *men*."

"No! I'm not like that." He thinks I'm some sort of a player. Me. I have zero game, minus-negative game. "I'm not like that at all."

"I didn't mean anything by it," he says. "I'm just talking shit. The minute you feel I'm insulting you, you can hit me. The Sanchez family is known for their power punches. Seriously, I'm not trying to play you."

I search his face to see if he's telling the truth. He sounds genuine. He doesn't look away and neither do I. But eventually I do. I'm starting to feel something for him but that's not a good thing. Nope. I grab my stuff to go.

"Oh. You're leaving already? I'll walk you," he offers.

"No, thank you," I say. "I think I can handle walking across a park."

"Can I call you, then?" he asks. "If it's cool with you."

"No." I sound annoyed although I don't mean to be. A part of me wants him to call but the other part knows what's up. "I'll see you around, right? Right."

I get up and walk away. I could act normal but no, I have to be dramatically backward. I'm crossing the street to the supermarket when Moises catches up to me and hands me a book.

"This is just a little something. Read it. I think you'll like it."

I saw this book on that first day I met him, right on the table. It's a collection of poems by Julia de Burgos, *Song of the Simple Truth*. Inside on the first page, I find his number and e-mail address with a note: *Anytime.*

CHAPTER 8

Jasmine waves me over as soon as I walk in the store from my morning break. I dread what "disaster" awaits me. Another busted jar of jelly? A group of rabid senior citizens searching for slices of ham? There's the always-popular duty of cleaning up the break room's disgusting microwave oven. With Moises out front, Papi's bent on making sure my time is fully occupied. Jasmine flaps her hands wildly. The task that awaits me must be epic. I don't care. I take my sweet time. Only thirty-eight days left until Nick's party. Although my lunch with Moises keeps replaying in my thoughts, I have to stay focused.

"Something's going down," Jasmine says when I finally reach her. "For real."

"What?" I ask.

"Shhh. Listen."

Even with the salsa music and the cash registers ringing, I can still make out Junior's fist slamming against the desk and Papi yelling at him. A third, quieter voice must be Oscar. From what I've witnessed, he's the calm, rational one. With Junior and Papi always at each other's throats, poor Oscar must spend most of his time acting like a referee.

Jasmine leans in and says, "Someone's stealing money and it ain't me because if it were, I would take enough to get the fuck out of here."

Jesus. I stare at the workers. Any one of them could be stealing, even Jasmine. I've seen her paycheck. She makes close to nothing. Some of these workers raise families with what they make here. Not sure how that's even possible. No wonder Papi's been on edge.

"*How long has this has been going on? You're looking at the damn books!*" Papi yells. "*We are not talking about pennies. This is a lot of money.*"

"*Fuck. Oscar is looking at the numbers too. Why don't you ask him?*" Junior says. "*Stop hounding me like it's my fucking fault and let's figure this out.*"

"*Como qué this isn't your fault? In the years I've had these mercados I've never had discrepancies. Not a one. I can account for every damn cent. Do you hear me?*"

"*Blame me like you always do!*" Junior yells. "*I can't do shit right no matter how many hours I work at this place. Can't wake up early enough for you. Can't manage the workers. It's never enough. I will forever be a failure."*

"How long have they been up there?" I ask.

"Ever since you went on break," Jasmine says.

Customers notice the commotion. This is becoming a serious problem. They need to tone it down. It's one thing to argue at home, enclosed where the shouting can be contained, but out in public? Mami would have a heart attack if she knew.

"Who would steal from us?" I ask. "I can't wait to find out so that we can haul their ass to jail."

"Bitch, it could be anyone! Do you see us living in luxury like you?" Jasmine says. "I'm not saying I'm stealing. I'm just saying you can't blame a person for trying to get theirs."

There is no "getting theirs." Papi works hard to provide us with everything. He lived in this neighborhood, got a job at this very supermarket and was able to save enough money to buy it from the owner. True, I've never had to deal with hard times growing up but we are not living in luxury. I wish. Jasmine justifies a crime simply because my family lives comfortably. We shouldn't be punished for that.

"What do you think, Rosa?" Jasmine yells to the cashier-ista at the next register. "Princesa is about to crack the case wide open like she's on *Law and Order*. She doesn't even know how to wipe her ass yet. Like this bitch never stole a thing."

Her words sting because the realization finally hits me. It was only a few weeks ago when Papi grilled me for taking his credit card. I did exactly what this thief did. Maybe I told myself I deserved the money. That being a Sanchez meant I should live a certain way. My nickname is Princesa, isn't it? I should get what I want when I want it. How is that different from what this thief is doing right now? I try to cloak myself with my justified anger but I'm a big hypocrite.

"Didn't you steal six hundred dollars?" Jasmine says. "Isn't that the reason why you're here?"

My shame grows with each comment Jasmine makes. Rosa snickers along with her. It's too much. I walk away from their cackles and Junior's escalating yells. I step outside and keep moving until I stop in front of the community garden. Two men sit crouched to the ground, working the dirt. I lace my fingers in the chain link fence and lean against it.

Every time I charged a purchase on Papi's credit card I knew it was wrong but my need to belong canceled any doubt. I had decided that I would no longer be the Princesa my parents want me to be. I would be Margot, a girl who could buy whatever she wanted. It wasn't based on reality but if I willed that person into existence maybe it could be. I felt so close to Serena and Camille with every purchase. Our dynamics shifted that day. I was happy until I got busted.

Papi couldn't understand why I would do such a thing.

Why take the credit card when he would have given me the money if I had asked? I didn't know how to answer him. There was no way I could explain how desperate I felt. Does the person stealing money from the supermarket feel the same desperation? Is that what propels them to steal? I can relate.

"Hey!"

Moises appears besides me. He playfully bumps his shoulder against mine. I can't shake this funk with my usual verbal vomit. I'm too upset to try.

"Hey," I mumble.

We just stand there.

"How's it going?" he asks.

I contemplate telling Moises. The burden would weigh less if I shared it with someone but that thought only lasts for a second. I don't know him and disclosing my family's drama to a stranger isn't what I was brought up to do. Instead I tell him everything is fine.

"Want to go inside?" Moises asks after a long silence. "I was going to pop in for a second. See what's growing."

"No, I should go back to work."

"All right. I will leave you with your thoughts, then."

He goes in and greets the two guys. After a few jokes, Moises drops his messenger bag and joins them in pulling weeds. Even with cars honking and a stereo blasting reggaeton nearby, the garden seems like an oasis, with rows of vegetables and so much green. It must be nice to work in a place where the focus is about growth.

Although Moises is on his knees working, every so often he looks my way. How does he do it? He's had a rough childhood, from what Jasmine told me, yet that doesn't stop him from always lending a hand. How does a person go from dealing drugs to pulling weeds? Maybe some people are born good no matter their circumstances. What if I was born to be selfish?

The gate to the garden is open. I could go back to the supermarket and feel bad. Try to avoid Jasmine and the rest. Worry about thieves stealing from my family's livelihood. Or I could step away from it. I surprise myself and head toward the gate.

"You changed your mind," Moises says. He introduces me to his friends. "Pop a squat and check these out."

He points to a row of green peppers. They're so bright and big.

"Willie here tells me they're due to harvest these bad boys next month. They make this hot sauce that will burn your tongue off," Moises says. "Do you have a green thumb?"

I've never grown a thing. Mami loves to garden and she's meticulous about it but she only grows for beauty. Everything about her garden is to show how perfect the Sanchez family is. The perfect house with the two perfect kids.

"No, I'm not good with living things." This makes Moises laugh. Sometimes I say things without thinking them through. But it's nice to see his smile.

"At least you're honest," he says. "Come take a look over here."

We slowly walk up the narrow rows.

"These blue flowers are called meadow heliotropes. You grind these up in a tea and they give you insight into the future," he says. "These are called dragon's calendula. If you smell them you will be cursed with bad breath forever."

"Do you even know what you're talking about?" I ask, laughing. He's making these names up and it's hilarious.

"No, but you believed me there for a second. I could tell," he says.

"Well, then. These are devil soapweed," I say, and join him. "Chew on these and you land right in hell."

"But why do you have to go so dark, though? All right. Let me see what we've got growing here." We take turns making up ridiculous names of plants that don't exist, laughing at our own creations and trying to one-up each other.

"These plants may look innocent." Moises points to a row of leafy greens. "But these are . . ."

"Greenavorous herbs." I jump in. "They turn your skin green if you touch them."

"Right. But only at night, like el coquí." He tucks his

chin and speaks low. "If you took a bite and turned into a coquí I would still be your friend. I'd meet you here at night and we could stay in the garden. I give you my word, Margot."

We're both goofing around but suddenly I feel shy. He likes me. I can see that and it leaves me feeling anxious, like I should say something super witty or sexy. I'm tongue-tied and because of that I make up an excuse to go back to the supermarket.

"Thanks for showing me around," I say. "It's nice here."

"Sure, anytime. I'll see you on the block." He walks back to Willie. I close the garden gate behind me. For a moment there I felt like myself. The hang-ups that usually tie me down were gone. I didn't think for a second how my interactions might seem to him. But it didn't last long enough before I realized my place. I take another look inside the garden.

Moises gestures to me. He meets me by the fence.

"Willie says lavender is a great way to deter the pests that like to eat their crop," he says. "I figured you could use some to ward off whoever is messing with your day."

He hands me a sprig of lavender through the chain link fence. The aroma is mild with a hint of camphor.

"It smells nice," I say. Then pause. "But why give this to me?"

He tilts his head.

"You are emanating sadness from miles away," he says. "I thought you could use a natural weapon to fight back. Besides, sometimes it's just about kindness. There are no strings, or flowers, attached. I saw them and thought of you."

Kindness when I need it. Moises, with his poetry books and his flowers, is making me fall for him.

"So . . . does it work instantly?" I jokingly aim the sprig at him.

"Aw, man! I left myself wide open for that one," he says. "I'm going to give that one to you because it was worth it. Later, Margot."

Although my mind is still weighed down by what's happening at the store, I can at least smell the lavender.

Inside, the screaming match has apparently ended and Jasmine is too busy dealing with customers to pay attention to me. I tuck the lavender in the pocket of my uniform jacket and grab a hairnet.

Papi usually drives us home a little before four to avoid traffic but not today. His office door has been closed, with either Oscar or Junior coming in and out. When I walked in to see if Papi was ready to go, he grunted no and said soon. It's five and I wait for him in the break room.

The daily check-in call to Serena was brief. They're spending their day on a friend's sailboat and the connection was spotty, which was fine by me. I'm not in the mood to act gleeful when my thoughts are consumed by money being stolen. There's already a fear of a new supermarket taking over our second location and now this. No wonder Papi is so worried and angry. Then there's Moises and the lavender he gave me. He was just being nice but it's hard not to make a big deal out of it in my head.

My thoughts turn to Elizabeth and that time when Junior lost his wrestling scholarship. The house was kind of unbearable with Mami and Papi raging against each other. My solution to avoid the cross fire was to schedule sleepovers at Elizabeth's house. Those times with her were the most fun we had before we went to separate schools.

I scan the old Instagram account WEARABLE ART and find the picture of us dressed as the Ronettes. Elizabeth painted a backdrop of a 1950s convertible and we posed in front of it. I couldn't stop laughing, which made our cat-eye makeup look more like crazy cat lady makeup. It seems so long ago. I miss playing dress-up and acting silly with Elizabeth. Camille and Serena are so into being adults that there's no room for weird. When did everything become so serious?

Junior storms into the break room. He slams open the refrigerator and takes a sip from a bottle he keeps stored way in the back. I better steer clear. Nothing but hate pours from him and I don't want to get spilled on.

"Where did you go for your break?" he asks.

"What do you care?" I say.

"I asked you a question. Someone said you were talking to some guy."

"Who said that? I can't believe this. Are you spying on me?"

He takes a long gulp from the bottle and wipes his mouth with the back of his hand. There are sweat stains on his favorite shirt. He didn't even bother shaving. Junior looks like a hot mess.

"I'm going to ask you one more time," he says. "Where were you?"

He grabs my arm. Hard.

"If I find out that you went out with that asshole out front, I'm going to kick your ass."

His breath reeks of alcohol. How insane is his life if he can't even wait to finish work to drink?

"I'm not explaining anything to you," I say. "And why can't I be friends with Moises? You were friends with his brother."

A flash of shock sweeps his profile. It's quickly replaced with anger. His grip tightens.

"Moises and his piece-of-shit brother are drug dealers. And no sister of mine is going to be seen with a thug. It's bad enough I've got to take care of shit in here but now I have to look after you too."

LILLIAM RIVERA

"Shouldn't you be worried about finding the person who's stealing money instead of wondering who I'm talking to?"

Junior's eyes are bloodshot but even in their bleariness I can see the saucer size of his pupils. He looks possessed.

"Let go of me, Junior. Let go!"

"What else did that motherfucker say about me?" he yells into my face. "What else? You're not hanging with them, you hear me?"

I can't stop the tears from rolling down my cheeks as I try to pull away. There was a time when Junior planned whole Saturdays for us. He called them Serious Sanchez Sábados. A movie, arcade games, whatever I wanted for dinner. The night always ended with a sundae so big that I could never finish it. It was our special day together. Where is the Junior who used to buy me sundaes? There's nothing left of that brother. This person who wrenches my arm acts like he wants to kill me.

"Let go, Junior," I say, wincing. "Please."

"Déjala!" Oscar enters the room.

Junior pauses, drops my arm, and pushes past Oscar.

"There, there." Oscar hands me a tissue. I'm so upset, it's hard for me to calm down. "He didn't mean it," Oscar adds. "He loves you. Es el stress."

That wasn't stress. I don't know what that was. Junior is out of control. Something is eating him up. It might be the job but I feel that there's something more and that somehow it's my fault. It's hard to keep tight the fleeting memories of when Junior was a decent brother.

"This work isn't meant for everyone." Oscar wipes the beads of sweat above his lip with a napkin. "There's so much to look after, and your brother wasn't born to do this type of work, but he tries."

"If he sucks at this job he should quit," I say. There are large red marks on my arm, evidence of Junior's "stress."

"Do you know how much your papi loves having you both here? The supermarket is your papi's life and he wants to share it with you." Oscar touches my shoulder. "Your father is thinking about your future. Junior will eventually be the owner. He wants you both to see how important el mercado is to the family. Entiendes?"

I nod. The supermarket may be in Junior's future but it's not in mine.

"Have you seen pictures of the kids?" Oscar tries to lighten the mood.

He pulls out a bulging, worn leather wallet and shows me pictures of his three boys, all under the age of five. The youngest, not yet walking, is the exact replica of Oscar. Pudgy and bald. The twins have grown so much.

"Son traviesos. Do you know what they were doing the other day?" Oscar says. "Jumping off the cabinet like they were Superman. Este got five stitches."

He couldn't be prouder of their dangerous antics.

"Having boys is hard," he says. "Just ask your father."

WHAT'S REALLY HARD, AN ABBREVIATED LIST

Running a marathon

Running a marathon in heels

Running a marathon in heels while breastfeeding a newborn

CHAPTER 9

My hands are numb from working in the cooler stocking the gallons of milk and juice. I walk outside to warm up with a nasty verse of a rap song stuck in my head, thanks to Dominic. He's good for that sort of thing. But it's not all bad. He did ask me for dating advice, somewhere to take his girlfriend on their four-month anniversary. When I told him to take her to this nice restaurant in the city he said, "Forget it. She ain't worth it." And that was that.

Facing the parking lot, I stand by the door and wait for my fingertips to defrost. I spot Oscar's minivan by the Dominican flag that dangles from the front mirror. The rest of the cars have various flags—Puerto Rican, Mexican—with the exception of Dominic's battered old Toyota. His car accessory is a picture of some half-naked girl. Papi's sedan sits in the only parking space with a tent placed to block the sun. Papi doesn't believe in flags, boxing gloves, or bumper stickers that proclaim patriotic love. He considers such displays low-class.

A car door slams shut. Loud and purposeful. Jasmine walks with her stomping heels. Whoever dropped her off honks the horn twice but she doesn't acknowledge him. She's very late but that's nothing new. What is new is that she has no makeup on. No red lipstick. No glittery blush. Even her nails are bare.

I step aside. Without her armor of makeup, Jasmine is even scarier. She draws nearer and I mutter a hello but avoid eye contact. She doesn't respond. Right before entering the supermarket, she stops. She's reluctant to go in. Instead, she sucks her teeth, pulls out a cigarette, and lights it up. The person who dropped her off revs his car and drives away.

"Motherfucker," she says.

"Is everything okay?" I ask.

"No." She blows smoke with force. "It's not."

While her cigarette dangles from her mouth, Jasmine pulls out a rubber band and gathers her hair in a tight ponytail.

"He keeps pushing the date but I want it done now." She flicks nonexistent cigarette ash to the ground. Sometimes Jasmine likes to talk to me but it's more like she's talking at me. I have no clue what she wants to get done.

"My demo!" she says, bothered when I don't respond quickly enough. "I'm ready to lay down the tracks. Enough songs for two albums but he wants me to wait. The fuck I'm going to wait."

The demo is Jasmine's obsession. She's always jotting down a verse or working with Dominic on a rap lyric for possible guest rappers. Everything rides on finishing the songs, on hitting big time. But how realistic is that dream? She might as well play the numbers. I've heard her sing. She's good but she's not Adele-good.

"I'm not like those other pendejas who will suck his dick for some studio time. I ain't the one." She inhales again and taps her heel at a rapid speed. "Don't let anyone steer you on the wrong path. I'm telling you right now. Men don't want you to succeed. They just want you down on your knees. But not me. I'm going somewhere. Believe it."

She scans the parking lot. It's as if I can see inside her head the different schemes and calculations to get out of here. It's how I feel but at least I've got Somerset. The super-market is a minor setback but come September, it will be just a blip in my year. What Jasmine has is a pop dream.

"Okay."

"What? Am I boring you or something?" She points at me. "You think I can't make it. Just because you're going to some rich white school doesn't give you the keys to the kingdom."

I can't take another person yelling at me, not after Junior's mental breakdown yesterday. Do I look like some walking target?

"It's not my fault your guy isn't finishing up your track," I say. "You should hire someone. Not everyone owes you or is out to get you."

But everyone here is definitely out to get me, to school me as if I have no clue about life. Even Moises with his poetry book. After going through the book, I felt so dumb. I didn't understand most of it. Was Moises trying to insult me in some cryptic way? Or was he being nice? I fear it's a little of both and that confuses me.

"Just throw money at the problem," Jasmine says. "It's how the Sanchez family rolls. Life as Papi's Princesa."

Jasmine scrutinizes me. She likes this, getting me riled up to see how far she can push me. It's a game.

"Money. Yeah, right," I say. "I work here just like you."

The word "money" feels so light in my mouth for a word that controls everything. Papi still hasn't mentioned the missing cash. I thought it would be the topic during dinner but he left soon after dropping me off at home. Something about having to go back to the supermarket to check the inventory. Mami didn't say much. She always clams up whenever Papi works late and it's been happening a few times a week. Even when I asked her about her latest flower arranging class she barely responded. I overheard her talking to one of her sisters in Puerto Rico but I couldn't make out the gist of their conversation.

"You're nothing like me. I don't got a papi helping me out." Jasmine jabs her finger into the air as if she's poking at an imaginary person. "I don't need handouts or pity from anyone, especially you. I'ma make it to the top by myself."

There's no way of getting anywhere by yourself. I need Serena and Camille. I went from having Elizabeth as my best friend to knowing no one. There are still moments when I play catch-up with the rest. Jokes are exchanged and I can barely giggle at the right pauses. Sometimes I even fail at that, laughing five minutes after the fact. I don't know what they're talking about half the time. Who are we supposed to like now? What's the right song I'm supposed to know the lyrics to? It's as if I'm being tested. Be funny. Be cute.

I follow Jasmine back inside. She heads to her register and I go back to the gallons of milk. Hidden behind the towers, it's easy for me to imagine Jasmine scowling at the customers. She punches the register keys as if she's hitting a punching bag. She's determined to bust out. It's the only thing we have in common.

"Margot, can you come upstairs?"

Papi speaks into the intercom. I'm summoned to the office.

"Dum, dum-dum-dum. Dum," Dominic says. "Dead Princesa walking."

"Shut up," I say, which cracks him up.

• • •

Papi sits at his desk, arms folded across his chest. The lunch Mami packed for him of rice and black beans with breaded chicken sits untouched. Junior stands by him, mimicking Papi. His sour face tells me all. He's spewing lies. I put my guard up.

"They tell me you've been seeing a boy?" Papi asks.

"Who is 'they' and what boy?" I answer.

I know full well who he's talking about. I can't believe this. Junior is a snitch.

"Ese muchacho." Papi points outside. The supermarket is facing a real crisis and they're both sitting and wondering whether I've shared a bench with a guy. This is ridiculous. I see what's going on. Someone steals from us and Junior throws me out like a curve ball to distract Papi from his mess. I won't make this easy for them. I'm going to take this interrogation nice and slow.

"What do you mean 'seeing' him?" I say. "He does have a table out front."

"Don't be a wiseass," Junior chimes in. "You're hanging out with a drug dealer."

"He's not a drug dealer. He's a community activist," I say. "And I'm not seeing Moises or anyone else."

Papi has a stern face. He's on Junior's side.

"You just need to open your legs once and end up like the rest of the girls here," Papi says. "Stupid and pregnant."

Papi's words are like blows to my stomach. I've heard him speak like this many times before with the guys who work at the auto repair shop next door. They talk about past girlfriends or women who live in the neighborhood. Whenever I appear within earshot, Papi stops out of respect. But now? He's lumping every single girl on this block with some sexist statement. How dare he say that girls are too dumb to think for themselves when it comes to sex? What about the guy? Look at stupid Junior. He fucks everyone and Papi doesn't bat an eye. No one does. I'm not dumb enough to allow some sweet phrases uttered by a random guy to magically open up my legs. I've never even had a boy call me at home and now I'm doing it. Papi's forgotten who I am.

"I can't have my daughter associated with títeres," Papi says. "You're supposed to learn about responsibility, not go out with drug dealers."

"He's not a títere and you know nothing about the girls in this neighborhood. Stop generalizing about them and Moises."

"It's already going around the neighborhood. How do you think I found out about you chilling with that bum?" Junior says. "If you don't put a stop to this now, it's only going to get worse."

"What the hell do you care?" I say. "Don't you have real problems to worry about, like finding the missing money or screwing the next cashierista?"

"See what I mean?" Junior says as if I've offered up proof of my spiraling fall from grace. "She's already changing her ways."

"Enough, Junior," Papi says. "Let me handle this."

"Handle it, because word gets around. If you can't control your own daughter, why would people trust us?" Junior leaves. I head to the door too. I won't stand here and be accused.

Papi stops me.

"Princesa," he says. "I'm doing this because I want to protect you. Because I love you. We both do. You understand that, don't you?"

Love. Everything he does is because he loves me? Sending me to work here and keeping me from the Hamptons. Accusing me of being a whore while Junior drinks and screws whoever he wants. That's some bullshit way to love.

"Don't love me, then."

He rubs his temple. The phone rings.

"I don't want to hear about you talking to him or any other guy. Do you understand? And that's final."

Papi picks up the phone. He's not protecting me. He's worried about his image and what people will say if they find out his precious daughter speaks to a former-drug-dealer-turned-activist. They can't control me. If they're so nervous about me ruining the Sanchez reputation, I'll give them something to truly worry about.

Before heading back to the gallons of milk, I search for Moises's phone number and send him a text:

Let's hang out. Just you and me.

A couple of minutes later, Moises replies with: Cool.

CHAPTER 10

The smell of sulfur is everywhere. A cherry bomb goes off. And then another. With each mini-bomb, I edge closer to Moises until the noise melts away.

"This is crazy," I say.

"C'mon," he says as we find refuge in a bodega.

Fear is a funny emotion. It can stop you dead in your tracks, plans squashed before they're realized. Or fear can put you on a path you had no intention of taking. I made a huge mistake texting Moises. No doubt about it. But once I sent it, there was no turning back. Actually, the text was easy. It was the seconds that followed, waiting for his response, that made me increasingly aware that I had made an error.

I didn't consult Serena and Camille. They would have advised me to play the good girl so I can meet them in the

Hamptons. I'm already on week number four, with six more weeks to end my supermarket ordeal. Instead, I'm on some dumb rebellion trip. Junior and Papi think I'm fooling around with a títere, then I'll fool around with a títere. It made complete sense at the time but now that I'm walking the streets with him, I'm not so sure.

He picks out mangos from a pile of mostly bruised fruit and two large bottles of water. I have no idea what we're doing or where we're going. The plan was easy enough to figure out. I convinced Papi and Mami that I was doing something with Elizabeth in the city. I then told Elizabeth that I would meet her and her friends at some point during the night. She was super excited. I didn't mention Moises. My parents were more than happy to direct me away from any "distractions."

I step around a crowd setting off bottle rockets and pray they don't throw one my way. Although the Fourth of July was a couple of weeks ago, the Bronx is on some sort of extended fireworks kick. Something to do with the Yankees doing well. I don't follow sports. I don't care. I protect my face from being blown off.

A little boy tosses a firecracker in front of me. He's shirt-less and proud of his skinny chest. The boy struts toward me again, ready to light up another one. His smile is much too wide. We need to get out of this madness.

"Where are we going?" I ask.

"It's not far. Just up the block," Moises says.

He hasn't said much since I met him at the other side of the park. Maybe he's trying to figure me out. I hope he takes me somewhere nice and safe to eat. These fireworks scare me.

Moises stops in front of an apartment building with black iron gates on every window and rusty fire escapes draped with clothes hung to dry. It's run-down. Pungent smells of fried food and weed permeate the hallway. We pass by each apartment and I hear boleros playing on a radio and couples talking loudly. Or arguing? I can't tell.

"This is it."

He pulls out a large set of keys. The door has a Jesus sticker with GOD BLESS THIS HOUSE written underneath. It looks battered, as if someone used a ram on it. Moises swings the door open and the first thing I see is a framed portrait of the Pope, President Kennedy, and Martin Luther King. To the right, there's a long passageway with several doors on each side. To the left, a large gilded mirror leans atop a matching gold table. A vase brimming with fake flowers sits in the center. The flowers are encrusted with dust. Everything seems old and cheap.

I wait outside the apartment. This isn't what I'm used to. I'm not that bold. I take a deep breath. This is only a dare, I say to myself, an adventure.

"Don't worry. She's at a church retreat. She won't be back till late."

An invitation to hang out means chilling at his apartment. Alone. This is how the night will go down. What was that thing Papi said? Will I see this thing through?

I step inside.

Sweat tickles my neck. The air is stifling. The tiny living room is so cluttered with furniture that there's barely any room to stand. There are small statues of saints and a bunch of wedding souvenirs displayed like trophies. Although I want to, I don't touch a thing. Whoever "she" is would notice.

"She likes to collect things," he says.

"Your mom?"

"No. I live with my aunt. My dad is somewhere in Puerto Rico. Mom is out of commission."

"What do you mean 'out of commission'?"

He pauses. "The last I heard she was smoking crack with some guy. I haven't seen her in a couple of years."

"Oh. That would definitely put you out of commission." I chuckle but there's nothing to laugh about.

He turns to me.

"Now that you've heard my shiny background, you still want to stay?"

"Why? Am I supposed to be scared or something?" I say.

"You're probably used to chilling with guys who come from money, two parents, a nice house."

He's judging me, addressing me in the same manner he used with Junior that day they almost got into it.

"You don't know what I'm used to," I say.

He keeps his gaze fixed on me. I try to hold the stare but quickly surrender. I feel the heat bounce off my cheeks. Things were a lot easier outside when all I had to do was dodge firecrackers. Now that we're inside, doubt circles around me.

We walk down the corridor and a ball of fur scurries past us, heading to the living room.

"What was that?" I ask.

"That's Midnight the cat," he says. "I wouldn't pet her though. She's pretty vicious."

We enter another room. Unlike the living room, this room is empty of furniture except for a flimsy white sheet that covers a mattress on the floor. A single bulb hangs from the ceiling. Posters of Malcolm X, Pedro Albizu Campos, and a bunch of other serious people cover the dingy walls. The room smells of dirty socks.

Moises removes a stack of books from atop a crate and lights a few sticks of incense.

"Take a seat," he says, and points to the crate.

A small breeze enters the room but not enough to make a difference. I keep my arms and legs crossed. I try not to move.

"Do you, um, sleep here?" I ask.

"Yeah. It's a place to crash until I can afford my own," he says.

"Oh."

I bite my fingernail. There are so many voices in my head telling me to leave. This isn't for me. Neither is Moises. What must he think of me when the only place he takes me to is his bedroom?

I walk over to a mirror where various snapshots are pressed against the frame. Moises names each person in the picture as if I'll remember.

"This is my crew, my panas," he says. "After things went down with my brother, they held me together. Freddie here, he's my right hand. He steered me away from some wild shit I was getting down with."

All I can think is that Moises stands way too close. This too is a challenge so I stay where I am and nod as he explains how important his friends are to him. How a bunch of suspicious-looking chicks saved his life. He smells of musk. I hold my breath and anticipate his next move. Can I be like those girls in the picture with their tank tops and cutoffs? They seem to know what to do, unafraid, grins flashing, curves showing. One hand firmly placed on their waist, hips popped to the side. They're so sure of themselves. But me, I don't dress like them or talk like them. There's nothing sexy about me. I'm completely at a loss. I sit back down on the crate.

Elizabeth sends me a text wondering what's taking me so long. Thankfully, she already had plans to meet with her friends at Central Park's SummerStage. I respond: Soon. I will let you know.

A blast from a cherry bomb outside startles me. I don't know if I can keep this up. Even Moises notices my anxiety.

"I got an idea," he says. "One sec."

He runs out and I hear him open and slam doors. He rummages for something. I pray he's getting ready to leave. Instead, he comes back and hands me a sleeping bag.

"Let's go."

"Where?" I ask.

"Trust me."

I don't know him but that doesn't stop me from following him up a few flights of stairs. What am I doing? It's like I'm pushing some imaginary boundary to see how far I will go. He pulls out another set of keys and opens the door and a soft breeze greets us. We're on the roof. From up here, I can really see the fireworks. It's as if neighboring blocks are communicating through loud bangs and sparkly lights.

"This is awesome." I peer down at the people on the streets scrambling for fireworks position. We can even see a couple of stars twinkling in the sky.

"No one is allowed up here," Moises says. "I help the landlord around the building so he gives me access."

He pulls out a blanket and spreads it out. I open the sleeping bag and lay it close to the blanket. Then Moises cuts open the mangos and we eat. When he's done, he lies on his back to watch the fireworks. I don't know what to do with myself so I just sit there and act as if this is a normal occurrence.

"Come look at the stars." He taps the empty side of the blanket next to him, a signal for me to join him. My heart pounds. I suck at this. I lie next to him but I can't just stare dumbly at fireworks. My mouth has to move. I turn to him and notice a long scratch on his arm.

"Where did you get that?" I ask.

"My aunt's cat. " He points at a small scar on my hand. "What about you?"

"I got that when I fell off my bike. I think I was ten." I point to my knee. "I got this one in Hawaii. I slipped off a rock. Your turn."

"I think that's it," he says.

"What are you talking about? What about that scar on your neck?" I lightly run my fingers across it.

He flinches.

I regret being so bold.

"You don't have to tell me if you don't want to," I quickly say.

He hesitates. "No, it's cool." He takes a sip from his bottle of water.

"I must have been around nine. My brother used to time me whenever I would go to the store for him. Once, I ran into my friend and started fooling around. When I got back,

Orlando told me the next time I took a detour he would tie me up by my neck. He showed me how he would do it. I ended up with this rope burn as a nice reminder to never be late."

Who does that? I've never heard anything so cruel.

"Jesus. You were just a kid," I say.

"Yeah, it's kind of fucked up. That's the Tirado family for you."

Moises tries to be a man about this story, to act as if what his brother did to him was okay, but there's no cause to. It's only us up here and the popping firecrackers. I stare at him and for the first time I don't look away. I place my hand over his.

"But you're not like your brother. You're different."

He slowly pulls his hand away.

"What makes you so sure?" Moises spits the words out as if I've unmasked some sort of hurt. Foolish to think my simple gesture could help him forget the memory. Even worse to believe I have a right to touch him.

"I didn't mean anything by—"

"Let me ask you something. Why did you send me that text after bailing on lunch?" he asks. "Are you slumming it? Seeing how the other half lives?"

This anger is not meant for me. I must have embarrassed him and for that I feel bad. But what he says still hurts and I'm a sucker for taking it. He can keep his mangos. I get up.

"There's this misconception that people from the South Bronx are always trying to get out." He continues with his rant. "But not everyone is stuck. Some people choose to live here. I saw the expression on your face when I took you to my room. You look down on me and my family."

Anger builds up inside me. We've gone from sharing something intimate to accusations I can't quite pin down. Anyone in their right mind would be shocked to see how he lives. He doesn't even sleep on a regular bed but on some lumpy mattress on the floor. There isn't anything wrong with wanting good things.

"Listen, Mr. Bronx." I defend myself. "Instead of wasting time trying to save others with your righteous attitude, why don't you buy a damn bedroom set? I'm so out of here."

When I reach the door, it's impossible to open. It's jammed shut no matter how much I pull. My grand exit falls like a dumb afterthought.

"Wait," Moises says. "Hold up."

"Fuck you!" I pull but nothing happens. I'm stuck on a roof with a guy who hates everything about me. "Open the door so I can get out."

"Hold up."

"No, open it!"

"Before I open it, give me a sec to explain," Moises says. "I'm sorry, Margot. For real, I'm sorry. That shit wasn't right. I said it because . . . I had no right to make you feel bad. I'm a jerk. Just because you got money doesn't mean you have everything. I fall into that mind-set, I want to decimate everyone around me."

He wants to peg me with everything evil. If you don't live like him then you're trying to be white or rich or something other than what you are. I don't even know what I am yet. I'm just maintaining, just like him.

"Look, I was surprised when you reached out," he continues. "I figured you're into playing games and I'd play along. I was wrong. I like you and although we come from different worlds, I want to connect. What I'm failing to say is that . . . let's hit the rewind button."

With that, he starts doing some crazy maneuvers. He walks backward. I try hard not to laugh but it becomes difficult when he starts to mouth words in reverse. After a while, I give in. I won't forget his hurtful actions but watching him act the fool eases things a bit. A tiny bit.

Instead of going back to the sleeping bag, he walks over to the edge of the roof. I join him but leave a sizable gap between us.

"My name is Moises."

He sticks out his hand. I should cut my losses and leave. I don't shake his hand but I accept his apology for now. His display is funny but I don't have to buy all of it.

"Don't talk to me like I'm some clueless person," I say. "I'm not looking for guidance from you or any guy, for that matter. This isn't a war and I'm not trying to attack you."

"Fair enough," he says. There's a pause filled with popping firecrackers. "Then what is it you want?"

Whoa. I thought I was placing boundaries like a mature person. Didn't think I would have to participate in real talk with him.

"Nothing. I don't want a thing," I say. My initial plans of using Moises to get back at Papi and Junior float away. "I just want to talk."

"Talk?"

"Yeah, don't be so shocked. Some girls just want to talk. I guess I'm different."

"A little," he says. "Did you read any of the poems by Julia de Burgos yet? There's a poem titled 'Yo Misma Fui Mi Ruta.' That poem sort of reminds me of you."

"Oh. Is that a good thing?"

"She writes about being her own person. How people try to push her in one direction because she's a woman, because of her class, but she refuses it. She's doing her own thing. I can see that in you," he says. "I'm surprised you've never heard of Julia de Burgos. I guess your school is too busy teaching you the same played-out subjects."

"Somerset is a great school," I say. "They offer a bunch of subjects regular public schools never do. What school do you go to?"

"I don't," he says. "I'm getting my GED."

He's not in school. At home, we have no option but to graduate and go to college.

"Not everything can be taught at school. You learn more from interacting with people." Moises tucks his chin in and then slowly looks up with a slight smile. "So, you want to make out? Naw, I'm kidding. Seriously, though, if you want to I'm here for that. I'll be your 'practice' until Nick sees the light."

My laugh is so loud, anything to cover my nervousness about him wanting to kiss me. There's definitely something about him. I can admit that. We look up and an explosion of fire takes over the sky. There's another explosion too. Elizabeth blows up my phone with texts. She wonders where I am.

"Your family knows you're with me?" Moises asks.

"Of course," I lie.

"And your brother is cool with it?" he asks.

"Junior is not my warden."

"Warden. That's a funny word choice."

"He's not always like that." It's one thing for me to be pissed off at Junior but I don't like it when others rag on him. So here I am mouthing the same excuse Oscar gave me a couple of days ago. "Sometimes Junior can be sweet. He's just stressed out."

"I can tell that you care for him, despite him being a dick."

"Don't call him that."

What is it about Junior that compels Moises to speak so strongly? I won't deny that my brother was a jerk to him but he is still my blood.

"Why do you hate him? Junior won't tell me a thing. What is it about you two?"

Moises turns around and leans against the edge of the roof. He's hesitating and that only increases my curiosity.

"In a roundabout way, Junior reminds me of my past and of my brother," he says. "And I probably do the same to him. Remind him of things he'd rather forget. Anyway, sometimes people just don't mix."

Before I can ask more questions, my phone vibrates again.

Change of plans. I'm so sorry I can't make it. Will explain everything tomorrow! Talk later. Have fun, I text back. Elizabeth doesn't respond and I know somewhere in the city she is angry with me. But I push that thought away.

We stay up on the roof and talk some more. Sometimes Moises goes off on a tangent about the injustices in the world but I reel him back in. He's used to fighting. We eventually move the conversation back to the sleeping bag, and the butterflies roll in my stomach. I've made it very clear. I'm here only to talk. Moises doesn't try to kiss me but why is it that I still want him to?

• • •

The sun shines brightly. Moises's arm is wrapped around me. He snores. There's no way of knowing how long we've been like this. I remember that the conversation moved from one path to the next. My eyes grew heavy but we kept on until I couldn't keep them open anymore and the fireworks no longer startled me. And now it's morning and I can see his scar and the stubble on his chin.

Moises opens his eyes. He groans and inches toward me. Very slowly. So close that I feel his breath on my cheek, until his lips are on mine and I'm forced to close my eyes too. His lips are soft and tangy from the mango. For a few seconds, I allow myself to enjoy being this close to him. This is new but I'm not supposed to feel anything for Moises. Not this kiss. Not a thing. His hand trails along the side of my neck, down to my back, and inches its way underneath my blouse. My virgin alarm rings for him to stop. Once he goes further I pull away.

"I can't," I blurt out.

"We can take it slow," he says. "I want to be with you and if that means holding hands, I'm cool with that. If it means more, I'm cool with that too. You feel me?"

"No, it's not that."

He stops cupping my face.

"Your boy Nick," he says. "Right?"

He's right about Nick. Moises doesn't hold anything good for me. He's just a dare.

THE EDUCATION OF MARGOT SANCHEZ

"I need to go." I stand and take in his serious face, which glows against the rising sun. He gets up and rolls the sleeping bag. I help him clean.

"I'll walk you to the train station," he says. If he's upset about what just happened he doesn't show it.

"You don't have to," I say, but I'm glad he does because maybe that means I'm not a total jerk.

The streets are covered with firecracker remnants. Crazy thoughts spin through my head: that I spent the night with him, that Elizabeth is pissed off, and that I'm going to get busted.

When we reach the train station, Moises pulls his Metro-Card and swipes it for me before I can stop him. When I tell him he doesn't have to wait he shakes his head as if I'm talking nonsense.

The train approaches the station. I don't know how to end this. What do I say without sounding like an idiot or a coldhearted person?

"Thank you for walking me," I say. "And for last night. It was fun."

The doors to the train open but before I step in, Moises leans in and gives me a kiss on the cheek.

"I'll see you around," he whispers in my ear.

I stare at him as the train pulls away.

CHAPTER 11

Mami lines up empty bottles on an outside table in front of the garage. It's eight in the morning and she looks refreshed. A determined woman on a mission to clean in tight jeans and heels. There must have been some kind of get-together last night with the neighbors. I tiptoe toward the front door.

"Margot, come here." Her hair is in a bun, a style I've tried to copy many times but never achieve. My curly hair refuses to be controlled. She's about to grill me. When I texted her the lie that I spent the night at Elizabeth's, she responded with orders for me to be home no later than eight. It's a test to remind me that I'm still paying for my crimes but I passed because I made it back on time.

"How was it?" she asks.

"Fine." I adjust my sunglasses. I wish they could conceal

my whole body and not just my eyes. I have to get to my room. Elizabeth didn't respond to any of my texts or phone calls this morning. I'm nervous that she'll turn up at the house and blow my cover. I need to reach her.

Mami motions to the housekeeper to tackle the other side of the yard. She always complains how Yolanda is never quick enough but Mami doesn't give her a chance. She has a gift of reaching disasters first. Mami sniffs the air around me and crinkles her nose. Then she sniffs again.

"Have you been smoking?" she asks. "I can smell it from here."

"What! Are you crazy? Smoking is disgusting. It's Junior you're smelling."

She crosses her arms.

"It's probably incense or firecrackers," I say. "There was a fireworks display last night."

"Well, it stinks."

"I don't stink. Anyway, we didn't do much of anything." My fingers twirl my charm necklace. I can't let her trip me up. "We checked out the concert and went back to her place. If you want, you can call her mother and ask."

Mami would never phone Elizabeth's mom. She hates to appear like an oppressive dictator compared to Elizabeth's parents. And how could she not? They allow Elizabeth to work in the city whereas I'm on lockdown.

"Leave that alone," Mami says, motioning for me to

stop fidgeting with the necklace. "Your papi and I want to go over that whole boy problem. . . ."

"There's no boy so there's no boy problem." I hate being the topic of discussion.

"Princesa, I want you to listen very carefully and try to understand where we are coming from. There's an old saying in Puerto Rico: Dime con quién andas y yo te diré quién eres. Do you know what that means?" she asks. "It means you can judge a person by the company he or she keeps. If you hang out with bums that makes you a bum too. Me entiendes?"

"I'm tired and I stink." I try to cut her off. "I need to take a shower."

Mami refuses to drop it.

"I understand how it happens," she says. "You meet a boy and maybe he's nice-looking. Maybe he notices you, pays you compliments, but those statements are only temporary. Don't be fooled. These sinvergüenzas only want one thing."

What is Mami talking about? Both my parents have a warped sense of reality, where girls are clueless fembots who will blindly follow any guy and boys are predators out to attack every single girl. Sometimes I feel like I'm living in a *Mad Men* episode.

"We sent you to Somerset so you can focus on school. You have a great opportunity. This summer job, although it wasn't my idea, it's for you to pay off your debt," she continues. "Don't mess up your future with one boy who decides to pay you some attention."

Little does she know how much Serena and Camille have influenced me on this evil path she keeps mentioning. Mami and Papi would straight-up kill me if they knew I'd spent the night with Moises. I can't stand here and listen to her give me advice on how to retain my angelic reputation when I reek of sin.

"I have to go to the bathroom," I say. "I have to go."

"Margot, don't walk away from me. We need to talk."

The clinking of the bottles lets me know that she's not following me and that's a good thing. My heart thumps so hard I guzzle down a whole bottle of water to push the rhythm back to normal. I leave Elizabeth a fourth message. I need her on my side. Before I can send a follow-up text, there's a knock on my bedroom door.

"Princesa, it's me." Papi's voice sounds like gravel.

I run around the room and open windows. "Yes?" I need to mask any lingering odor from last night.

"Open."

"I'm about to take a shower." I hold the door only slightly ajar.

"The door. Ahora." He enters with a steaming cup of black coffee. His face is puffy and there are bags under his eyes. There must have been some heavy drinking last night while I was on a roof with Moises. Papi removes the clothes tossed on my bed and carves a space to sit.

"Did you enjoy yourself last night?" he asks.

"I did." I position myself next to the window and pray that Moises's musk oil evaporates off me. "I have to take a shower."

"Oh." Papi stands up, confused. He still holds a dress in his hand. "Bueno, I came to talk to you about that boy."

"Forget it. I spoke to Elizabeth about it. He's not from around here so I shouldn't talk to him. No big deal."

"Good. I'm proud of you. That's a sign of maturity," he says. "You'll eventually see that we were right."

Papi is pleased. The world is right now that Princesa is back to being his innocent daughter and that pesky boy is no longer a menace. If he only knew. Weird how my mango kiss happened only a couple of hours ago but a kiss is nothing. And that kiss in particular was a mistake.

"Margot, Elizabeth is here!" Mami yells from outside. Finally! I hope Elizabeth keeps her mouth shut. We've been so out of sync. I can't expect her to keep track of my lies.

"Hurry up and come upstairs," I yell back, and then turn to Papi. "Do you mind? Privacy, please."

Elizabeth arrives out of breath and sweaty in jogging clothes. I try to read her but she offers nothing but a blank expression. Since Mami hasn't screamed murder, I think I'm in the clear.

"Princesa won't tell me what she did last night," Papi teases. "What secrets are you girls keeping?"

Elizabeth laughs nervously. I watch as she opens her mouth to respond but stops. She needs to keep quiet.

"It's good seeing you girls together. Elizabeth, help Margot out. She's having a rough week at work."

"Ay, Papi, Elizabeth didn't come over to talk to you. Go already!"

I push him out of the room. Then I lock the door.

"Where were you last night?" Elizabeth asks. "I sent you so many texts."

I shush her. Papi could still be by the door. I can't take any chances. Besides, what is the big deal?

"I couldn't make it," I say. "Don't look at me like I killed someone."

"You should have told me," Elizabeth says. "I was freaking out. I almost called your parents."

She chews on a strand of blue hair. Elizabeth and I have never done anything bad. Good girls for so long. The boldest action she's taken is this recent dye job. When I told her I got caught stealing Papi's credit card, she couldn't believe it. She didn't understand why I would do such a thing, especially since Papi is never stingy with money. It was wrong to even tell her.

"I was with a friend," I say. "I'm sorry. I just lost track of the time."

"Who? Someone from Somerset," she says in anger. She can't hide her disgust. This is why I keep my two worlds separate.

"No, not Somerset."

She eagerly waits for details but I hold back. I don't know why. Maybe if I share my moment on that roof the event becomes tarnished. Misunderstood. Or maybe I don't want to be judged by my actions, good or bad.

"First you make me lie and now you won't even tell me what happened," Elizabeth says. "Why do I bother?"

She gets up to leave.

"It was some stupid boy and nothing happened," I blurt out. "We talked, that's it."

Elizabeth is disappointed that I didn't share any of this with her until after the fact.

"What boy?" she asks. "Do Serena and Camille know about last night?"

I shake my head. Not telling them earns me some points but not enough.

"Why weren't you up-front with me? I would have covered for you no matter what," Elizabeth says. "Sometimes you act as if we're strangers."

"If I had told you I was planning to hang out all night with some boy you've never heard of you would have told me I was crazy."

"You are crazy," she says, then pauses. "But I would

have covered for you. We've got each other's back, no matter what. Remember? Or has that changed?"

I don't bring up that time she abandoned me for her new friends during those first weeks at Somerset. Elizabeth had an immediate circle of friends while I couldn't figure anything out, not even how to open my new locker. I don't mention that. She thinks I've stopped being her friend but it was Elizabeth who pulled away first.

"I didn't make up this whole story while your mom grilled me with questions for nothing," she says. "I want details."

"It's just a guy who lives near the supermarket. Nothing serious," I say. "And we weren't alone. It was more of a block party with people I didn't know. My parents don't want me to talk to anyone from that neighborhood. I needed to make something up."

She squints at me. "Well . . . was he at least cute?"

"Yes, but he's definitely not my type." At least that part is true. "Sorry I wasn't up-front with you."

Elizabeth lets go of some of her disappointment. I don't want her to be mad. I know we haven't been close for some time but I still care about her.

"Well, you owe me twice now. The Boogaloo Bad Boys are playing later this week. Come with me," she says. "I'm dying to see them live. It will be fun."

When she tells me the concert is in some park in the

South Bronx I almost bail. It's like forces conspire to keep me there no matter how hard I try to leave. And the band? A mash-up of salsa, rap, and reggae, music I used to love back in the day. Now I take my musical cues from Serena and Camille. They like the latest bad-girl pop stars, the ones with the super-tight clothes and sugary lyrics that don't quite make sense with their naughty image. There's no flavor to the music but I can play along with their tastes.

"Can't we go see someone else? I don't like the Boogaloo Bad Boys."

"What are you talking about? You used to love Fuego when he was the lead singer of the Cumbia Killers. It's the same guy."

"Yeah, but I don't anymore. Let's see who else is performing." I go to my computer and search for another concert.

"Sarah Sez is playing at SummerStage. Let's go see her."

"No way. I hate those wannabe rappers. I can't believe you even listen to that junk. It's not even real music, just Auto-Tune," she says. "I perform this grand feat for you and you can't even come with me to see Boogaloo. They're only playing that one day."

"Okay," I say. "Okay, I owe you. I'll go."

"Yes! Since it's on Saturday, we can meet here and ride our bikes to the train station. It will be like old times."

When we were younger, Elizabeth and I would take to our bikes every weekend. She followed me through alleyways and streets, places our moms told us never to go. We acted like sisters on the run. I was always in front, pushing Elizabeth to go to sketchier areas.

I wonder if I'm running ahead of her. Maybe Elizabeth can't keep up. It's not my fault I have Somerset now. I'm making decisions about my life without her.

"What time do they go on?" I search the concert online. I won't diss her even if seeing the Boogaloo Bad Boys in concert is no longer my thing. "We'll meet here at eleven a.m. Does that work?"

"Let's dress up in their colors," she says. "Black and gold."

"I said I was going. No one said anything about dressing up."

"You used to love dressing up. Oh well, I'm dressing up." She does some stretches. "Don't forget. Saturday at eleven a.m. And if you're bored later today, come over. I'm working on some new paintings."

Whenever she starts a new project, Elizabeth will paint through the night. Her internship at the museum must inspire her. What does working at the supermarket inspire me to do? Go off with Moises. I'm sure it's not exactly what Papi had in mind.

"I'm too tired," I say. "And don't worry, I won't forget. You're going to keep sending me texts to remind me. Right?"

"You better believe it," she says, then leaves.

Before I even hit the shower, I receive a text from her.

Boogaloo baby! Can't wait.

CURRENT MOOD LIST

Slightly annoyed

Sleep-deprived

And every time I think of Moises—confused

CHAPTER 12

Before getting on Skype, I paint my face and put on a rose-colored top with a chunky necklace. My complexion is too pale so I create a little magic with the lighting in my bedroom. Mood lighting always works.

I missed my last couple of check-in texts with Serena. She decided we needed a Skype session. This is new to me and I'm nervous. I don't want to be criticized for wearing the wrong color eye shadow. I can never be flawless enough.

Camille caresses her collarbone. Her hair is even blonder from the sun. She covers her freckles with makeup but they still peek out, which is a shame since I think girls with freckles are pretty. I made the mistake of saying that to her once and she practically jumped down my throat, complaining that it was because of her dumb Irish side of the family she has these ugly marks on her face. Camille is also angry at her nonexistent "fat" ankles, inherited from her father, and her thin lips, a gift from her mom's side of the family. It's hard to be sympathetic. Camille already has a personal trainer and she plans to plump her lips when she turns eighteen.

"She almost lost her top!"

Serena sits next to Camille in a bright pink bikini top that shows off her olive skin. She recounts what happened at a party last night. Another event I missed. Serena doesn't have as many hang-ups as Camille when it comes to her body. Her parents are Serena cheerleaders, always singing her praises. I see this just from following her Facebook page. Her mother uses emoticons like they're about to expire. I don't think Camille's parents ever give her much public love. She rarely talks about them, only when she's rattling off what awesome place they're visiting. Her parents seem too busy living that glamorous life.

"What a skank!" Serena says. "She did it on purpose."

It's hard to concentrate. The last couple of days at work have been the same ol' routine with one exception: Moises hasn't been around. Is he avoiding me? I'd imagined seeing him and exchanging knowing glances. Or maybe having to explain to him that we could only be friends, that the other night was a fluke, but I haven't had the chance. The space in front of the supermarket has been empty.

"Are you listening?" Camille asks.

"Of course I'm listening. The girl is a total skank," I say. "She's the queen of the skanks."

Camille's in the foulest mood. She's on day three of a seven-day juice cleanse, in preparation for Nick's party. Last Christmas, she forced us to do a three-day juice cleanse. Although I told them I was doing it, I snuck in food whenever I could. When we did the big "weigh-in," I'd gained a pound. Camille accused me of cheating. No amount of juicing or preppy clothes will ever do away with my curves. It doesn't matter how hard I try to camouflage them, they still sneak out.

"Is Margot sucking face with anyone?" Serena giggles. "Is that why you're not paying attention? You did disappear on us a couple of days ago."

"No, not really." I don't want to mention my pathetic exploits. They aren't interested in them. It's not like my moment with Moises can compare with their pool parties.

"She's lying," Camille says. "Who are you tonguing? You can't possibly be working at your father's store the whole time."

I remind her that I'm not working at a store but a chain of supermarkets. Presentation is everything.

"Sorry, I mean supermarkets," Camille says. "So, what have you been doing to make yourself look good? What's your angle?"

Camille wants to trademark that phrase. It's on constant repeat. Her mother is the owner of an interior design firm. Clients are super-rich celebrities and fashion designers. It actually sounds like a dream job. Camille's mom has taught her the importance of creating buzz that will leave an impression, hence the "what's your angle" question. I don't want them to think I've kept myself completely secluded like some reject.

"My angle? I'm not doing anything serious, just keeping things casual." I hesitate but they want more.

"Talk!" Serena yells.

"Okay. Okay. There is this one guy."

"Oooh, you whore! You've totally been holding out on us!" screams Serena. "Who is he?"

"It's no one special," I say. "Just some local."

Camille scrunches her face in disgust. Big mistake. I should never have said "local." Even with the clumsy Skype connection, I can tell I'm losing points. I have to spruce up this story or I won't hear the end of it.

"I don't have much to pick from," I say. "The selection is pretty slim. But he's fine, was fine. I mean he's good-looking enough."

"What's his name?" Camille asks.

There's no doubt that as soon as I tell them they'll look him up online. Scrutinize him. Analyze Moises from head to toe. I could make up a name but that would be ridiculous. I better come clean. They just want a visual. They'll never meet him.

"His name is Moises Tirado."

Serena immediately takes to her phone. Camille sips her green kale juice and waits. The image that pops up of Moises is of him at what looks like a community rally. He holds that infamous clipboard and pen. The picture isn't close enough for them to see his scar but he does have that beaded necklace he always wears.

"Hmmm-hmmm. Nice beads," Serena says. Serena wears a similar necklace but she purchased hers during a safari she went on with her parents a couple of years back. Her father is a corporate lawyer. Big-timers. I think Moises's beads are made of plastic.

"He has beautiful eyes," I say. "They're dark brown and really intense. He's smart. Total body." I push too hard trying to sell him but even they can't deny how good-looking he is.

"He does have a nice body," Camille concedes. She puckers her thin red lips. "But he doesn't have much style."

The tension in my neck increases. I don't want to lose any social standing.

"How did you meet?" Camille asks.

"He collects signatures in front of the supermarket," I say. "He's a community activist."

"A community activist. Like rallies and demonstrations?" She caresses her long extensions. "Interesting."

Camille is not impressed. The more I talk the worse Moises seems.

"He gave me a book of poems," I say. "Anyway, we kissed. That's all."

"Ooooh, poetry. That's pretty hot. Are you sure that's all you did?" Serena says. "Anything else you want to share with us? Did anything pop off? You better tell because we have ways of finding out."

"There's nothing to say. I swear. We kissed. I was slumming it."

Jesus. Slumming it. That magical night between us is quickly betrayed with two words. Just like that. It's what Moises accused me of doing and here I am tossing him aside because I'm too scared to admit anything honest and real to Camille and Serena. If I present that side I'm left vulnerable. My role in our trio is to follow and copy. That doesn't include sharing anything of depth.

But what exactly am I winning by tearing Moises down like that? If I'm honest with myself, I'm left with this revelation: I don't fit in with them and I don't fit in with Moises. The last time I felt completely like myself was back in junior high with Elizabeth. But now Elizabeth and I are out of sync. So where do I stand? It's easier to lie and hurt someone who isn't present. Serena and Camille are in front of me now. I'll focus on them. It's wrong what I said but I'm too gutless to take the words back.

Camille finishes her juice. She's bored. Time to move past Moises.

"Any word on Nick's party?" I ask.

"It's happening. August twenty-first. Are you going to be here?" Camille says. "That is, if you're not too busy swapping spit with some guy."

"Of course I'll be there," I say. Nick's party lands on week number eight of my supermarket imprisonment, which means it's only a little under a month away. Papi didn't technically give me the green light but I will work my magic somehow. I will be in the Hamptons, trying my best to align myself with the girls and with Nick. "I won't miss his party."

"If you get an invite," Camille says.

Oh. I thought I had an in already.

"Why wouldn't I?"

"Well, you did promise to spend the summer with us and then that whole drama went down with your parents," Camille says. "I don't know if Nick will remember who you are. It's not like you're here to remind him."

My face drops. What am I supposed to do about that? Hire a plane and write it across the sky that MARGOT IS STILL HERE!

"What should I do? Do I send him an e-mail?"

"Camille is teasing." Serena nudges Camille, who laughs.

"Of course you got an invite," Camille says. "You're with us. Don't worry about it."

If Camille ate more, she wouldn't be so mean.

The girls head out to some bonfire. Another Saturday night and I'm home with no plans. There's nothing to do but beautify myself and erase the pit of ugly inside me for denying Moises.

"Mami, have you seen my tweezers?" I yell from the upstairs bathroom. She's at it again. Rearranging the bathroom medicine cabinet and moving things around. I can tell by the amount of cleaning products she's used that something is bothering her. She's been fixating on keeping the house in order. Snapping at Papi, and sometimes even snapping at Junior. When she starts doing that, I know it's serious.

The house is clean but the supermarket is falling apart, what with money being stolen. Mami argued with Papi this morning before he left for work. She wanted him home for dinner. He said this mean thing about paying for another class for her to take. It was a cheap shot. He can be so cruel to her.

"I put them here." Mami hands me a new crystal case from atop a shelf. It's much too extravagant for the over-the-counter tweezers I buy. I start to work on my forsaken brows. Mami decides my beauty challenge is a spectator sport.

"What are you doing? You have to pluck in the direction of the growth." She grabs the tweezers from my hand and pulls my face closer to the light. Even though she's spent the day cleaning, she still has makeup on. Her long dark eyelashes are even longer with mascara. Mami's older sisters taught her how to wear makeup and she taught me but I had to unlearn some of her lessons since caked-on paint isn't "natural-looking" enough for Somerset.

"Please don't overpluck," I say. She clucks her tongue, insulted by me bringing up the obvious.

Sometimes it's hard for me to imagine Mami my age. There aren't that many pictures of her as a kid. I know she was poor and that they lived in a small town. I know she met Papi there and he whisked her away to New York. She was the last to marry in her family, already in her midtwenties. Papi likes to joke that she was the old maid. Sometimes his jokes are not funny.

"Mami, what were you like as a teenager?" I ask. "Did you have a lot of friends?"

"I had my sisters and my cousins." She sets the tweezers down and lightly runs her finger across my brow. "I was never alone."

"But what about boyfriends? Did you have guy friends?"

"No, Princesa. There's no such thing as guy friends. Ese concepto es Americano," she says. "Papi was the only boyfriend I ever had. I met him and then we had Junior and later you."

She purses her lips, picks up the tweezers again, and concentrates on my other eyebrow. Papi took her away from the people she was closest to and moved her here. It must have been scary. When Elizabeth wasn't able to go to Somerset I had to fend for myself. I can relate to being alone in an unwelcoming space. Weird thing is that Mami has her classes and her friends from the neighborhood. Why does she choose to stay home and be sad? It wasn't that long ago when Papi used to take her out to romantic dinners. They would even watch their favorite singers perform, but I can't remember the last time they did that. She once told me that the first concert Papi ever took her to was to listen to Cheo Feliciano sing. She still has the gold dress she wore that night. There's a picture of them together that sits atop her bureau.

"Is everything okay between you and Papi?"

She sets the tweezers down again. "Of course. What makes you ask that?"

"You guys argue every day. You seem so down."

She holds my face with her slightly cold fingertips. We have the same eyes and at this angle, I can see even more of a resemblance.

"We are fine," she says. "Don't worry your head. You're young. Let the old people clean up their messes."

It would be nice if I had the type of mother-daughter relationship shown on television, where the mom is always there for the daughter and they share long discussions on serious matters. But those relationships probably only exist on sitcoms.

Can't she see that I'm not young anymore? There's no way I can talk to her about my feelings for Moises and Nick. She would never understand. Mami comes from the old school of thought where guys are considered the enemy until they gallop to rescue and marry you.

"There you go," she says, and places the tweezers back in the glass case. "Perfect. And leave your necklace alone."

Whatever is upsetting Mami she will never share. I will do the same and keep Nick and Moises hidden.

COUNTDOWN TO NICK'S PARTY (29 DAYS LEFT)
Create vision board of fashion selections for Serena and Camille
~~Shape those brows~~ Keep them shaped
Straighten out the hair
Practice what you will say when you see Nick

CHAPTER 13

In between taking deli orders, my eye drifts over to where Moises should be. His partner is handing out brochures and Moises is not around. How many days since the roof? I tell myself not to count. Instead, I count the weeks. It's the beginning of week number five. The halfway mark. I've made roughly twelve hundred dollars. Only twenty-six days left until Nick's party. I can do this.

"Come with me to get a slice," Jasmine says.

I look around. Is she really asking me to go out with her? "Me?"

"Yeah. Who the hell else am I talking to?"

"I already have my lunch." Jasmine usually eats with the other cashieristas. They never ask me to join them. Why do I feel like I'm being tricked?

"Don't give me that." She taps loudly on the deli's glass

window. Her nails are painted blood-red. "Fuck. You'd think I was asking for a kidney."

"No tapping on the glass," Roberto warns.

"Don't yell at me!" Jasmine's voice drowns out everything around her. She catches me looking out the window and refocuses her wrath. "Oh. I'm sorry. Are you waiting for a better offer?"

Did Papi send Jasmine to distract me from Moises? Seriously. I thought that drama was behind us. This could be a test to make sure I'm through with him. Jasmine is a spy and I'm going to have to treat this lunch like some undercover mission. Anything to keep my record clean in time for my only trip to the Hamptons.

"Fine. I'll go with you."

I struggle to keep up. The streets are jammed with people as if everyone decided to go outside. An elderly lady with Coke-bottle bifocals and a thin housedress walks in front of us pushing a cart filled with laundry. The old lady jerks to a stop. Her cart is lodged in a crack on the sidewalk.

"Don't you know how to walk?" Jasmine says.

"Ay, este carro." The old woman mumbles to herself, her confused look magnified by the thick glasses. I try to help her but Jasmine pulls me away.

"Jesus, Jasmine. What's the big rush?" I say to her. "She can use a hand."

"Give me a break. Stop acting like a Girl Scout."

This is the person I'm breaking bread with? Jasmine is so out of control. I better eat my slice super fast or I'm bound to get stung by her vicious tongue.

"Todo eso es tuyo?" says a leering man who leans against a parked car. "That juicy ass can't all be yours."

"Fuck you!" Jasmine yells. She doesn't even wait to verify if the guy is talking to her. He could be talking about my ass, although my long blouse basically covers it. I turn to look at the man. He slaps his knee. After his laughter subsides, he responds with additional X-rated declarations of booty love. We barrel through.

Before entering the pizzeria, Jasmine stares at her profile in the window.

"I'm getting so fat." She has put on some weight but she doesn't wait to hear whether or not I agree with her. She takes one last drag of her cigarette and walks in.

The place is packed. A couple of cops are stuffed in a booth, their guns dangling by their sides. A family takes over another booth with one kid screaming for ice cream while a cute young couple shares an extra-large cup of soda.

"What can I do for you?" the man behind the counter asks.

"What do you think?" Jasmine says. "Give me a slice and don't give me that oily one right there. I want it hot."

"All right, all right," he says. "Take it easy. What can I get you?"

"I'm trying to be healthy," I say. "I got to look cute

in a bikini. Pizza is not cute." The guy behind the counter looks bothered but I honestly can't decide. "I should order a salad."

"Hurry up!" Jasmine barks. "You act like you're reading the Bible. It's pizza."

"Jesus." I can't even with this girl. "I'll take a slice. Thank you."

Jasmine plops down at a booth. She scans the restaurant. She gives the young couple the once-over and taps a straw until the cover tears off. If Jasmine would tone down the anger, she would look pretty, but everything about her is hard-core. Even her overplucked eyebrows exaggerate her pissed-off demeanor. Is she ever sweet or nice? I can't say. I've never seen her that way. I'm not even sure if she likes me but here I am sitting across from her.

"Tell me about that fancy school you go to. Is it true MC3's kids go there?" Jasmine watches the grease stain spread across her paper plate.

"Yes, but they're older than me so I don't know them." MC3 is a rapper and his twin daughters attend Somerset. They're super popular and way out of my league. They're even more popular than Camille and Serena. The girls are nice, which makes it hard for anyone to hate them.

Jasmine shrugs and eyes my charm necklace. "Who gave you that?"

I always forget that I have it on. I never take it off.

"My mom, for Christmas."

"Every time I see your mother, she acts as if I owe her money." Jasmine speaks with her mouth full of cheese. "She's so stuck-up. I bet she doesn't even cook for your pops."

"She cooks for him but why does that even matter?" I say. "That's so old-fashioned. Does your mom cook for your dad?"

Jasmine huffs. "He didn't stay long enough to find out. Mami always tells me you have to take care of the house, cook, do everything or you'll be alone but she couldn't even keep her man. What a dumb ass. Your mother's dumb too. I would never leave my man alone with a bunch of girls."

"What are you talking about? Papi's not like that. Besides, those cashieristas are ugly. Can you imagine him with Ana?" Ana is one of the oldest workers in the supermarket. She has wrinkles upon wrinkles and a mole that enlarges every time I locate it on her neck.

"How do you know for sure he's not with Ana? You're not with him every second. Shit, maybe I'm fucking him."

What a horrible thing to say. What does Jasmine know? Not a damn thing about my father. If anyone's fucking around it's my brother. He's screwed everyone and everything in that store, plus the staff at the other location. Jasmine told me they made out once but they never took things further. He was too much of a child is what she said.

Wait. What if Jasmine and Junior are screwing and this is her weird way of being nice? I've had that happen before. Girls sidle up to me to get closer to Junior. I need to eat this pizza quick because I do not want to be a pawn in Jasmine and Junior's tragic love story.

Jasmine grabs the red pepper shaker and dumps some on her slice. She covers what's left of the pizza with a blanket of red dots.

"You ever been pregnant?"

"No way," I say. "I'm not that stupid."

"You don't have to be stupid to get pregnant. That shit happens all the time." She points her long red nail at me, the one with the gold hoop at the end. "You a virgin?"

"No, ummm, not really. You know . . . I've done stuff."

"Oh? I guess that makes you an expert."

"Yeah, well, I'm not trying to have a baby." Then it hits me. I study her face. It's not like she's glowing or anything. Just the same old scowl. But what if . . . "Are you pregnant?"

She rolls her eyes as if her predicament should have been obvious.

"I haven't gotten my period and I've been doing everything I could. I even went on that roller coaster ride Nitro in Great Adventure twice to see if it would do anything."

Oh my god, is it Junior's? Is this what this whole thing is about? I can't even form the sentences to ask because my head is about to explode. I don't want to know.

"Have you spoken to the, umm, guy?" I ask. "He can probably help you."

"It's so freaking easy for you to say," she says. "That's probably the way it goes down in your world. People talk to each other. I can't talk to him. I'm just his chilla, a dumb trick fucking him."

Jasmine snatches one napkin after another. She wipes her hands and tosses the crumpled paper on the table. I don't know where to look, definitely not at her. She hasn't said it's Junior. It's probably not him. It could be the music producer. Or some other guy from the block. Or Junior. It could totally be my brother. What an idiot.

"You're not going to keep it, are you?" I whisper.

"Maybe I will." She rubs her hand even harder. "He's got money so he can take care of both of us. I won't have to work at that place anymore."

Leave it to Jasmine to turn being pregnant into her golden ticket. She's not even thinking about the baby. I can't sit here and act as if I'm cool with her scheme.

"Don't take this the wrong way." I choose my words carefully. "But I think what you're doing is messed up. Using a guy just because he has money."

Jasmine stops in midrub and throws the napkin on the floor. "Like you've never done anything wrong, sneaking around behind your papi's back with Moises."

"I'm not seeing Moises."

She cocks her head in disbelief. "It is so obvious something's going down. You can't lie for nothing. I see the way he scopes you out. And you do the same. You're either seeing the idiota or trying to. Which one is it?"

Her face is like a wall, impenetrable. She won't break her resolve for anything. I'm not seeing Moises but there's no point in explaining this to Jasmine. She's made up her mind.

"That shit is funny. Papi doesn't want little Princesa dirtying herself up with some hood rat. Maybe I should tell him. It would wake his ass up to reality."

"Stop playing," I say. "Don't even joke about that."

"Everyone thinks you're such an angel but you're as fucked up as the rest of us. At least people see me and know where I'm coming from but you, you're just a two-faced liar."

"Well, at least I'm not stupid enough to get pregnant."

The silence that follows kills me. I want it to be filled with a loud elevated train rumbling by, a shot, anything. The warlike stare Jasmine throws is the same one she gave right before she found out a neighborhood girl was talking about her behind her back. I hold my breath and wait. But instead of grabbing my hair and slamming my head into the table, Jasmine suddenly smiles.

"We're two pendejas falling for guys we can't have. Fuck it."

I let out a sigh of relief.

"Moises is not like the other guys I know."

I can't believe I just admitted that. Where did that even come from? Moises is not in my plans and here I am gushing to Jasmine like a fool.

"I'm just saying . . . He's smart. Different."

The kiss. The night on the roof. It happened. Telling another person makes that night real and that's not a bad thing. It's not like Jasmine will tell Serena and Camille.

"We're just friends," I add.

"Yeah, friends. That's how I started out. And now look at me."

I stop talking and finish my slice.

At work, two people accuse Jasmine of overcharging. I can tell she's making rookie mistakes. Within minutes after that, she's involved in a shouting match with a customer over the price of avocados. I walk over from the deli to defuse the situation but it doesn't help. The woman wants to speak to the owner.

Papi comes down from his office and apologizes. He sweet-talks the sour-faced lady and offers her a free gallon of milk. She happily accepts.

"You should go home," he tells Jasmine.

"I didn't want to be here anyway!" She throws her smock to the floor and storms out, leaving behind a line of impatient customers.

To leave like that at the beginning of the evening rush,

I'm sure Papi will fire her on the spot. He fired a cashierista last week for giving him attitude when she took too long of a break. But instead of yelling at Jasmine to clean out her locker, Papi picks up the smock and folds it over his arm.

"I thought I had only two kids," he jokes, elbowing a man waiting to pay. The small vein on his forehead throbs.

"Do me a favor and bag these." He hands the avocados to another cashierista and goes back upstairs. Something is definitely going on. Papi must know Jasmine is pregnant and it's the reason why he's being lenient. It totally makes sense.

"It's about time." The lady snatches the bag. So rude. I've started to direct people to other registers when Junior pops up. Leave it to him to make an appearance when the coast is clear.

"Jasmine left," I tell him.

"Too bad," he says. "Have you seen Papi?"

"Don't you care about Jasmine?" He can't be that heartless.

"She can take care of herself," he says. "I got to talk to Papi. I think I know how we can turn our problems around. Instead of bugging out over the new properties being built, we should invest in one. There's a site for a new restaurant and bar. We can get in on it before someone else does."

Papi will not invest in some restaurant. Besides, what does Junior know about running one? Absolutely nothing. He's so desperate to win Papi over, to show that he's more than just the son who flunked out of college. Junior pursues flashy ideas that need lots of money behind them to live. I don't see Papi being game. Not now.

"What do you think? I already got a name: Sabor, a Sanchez Bistro."

Do I tell him the truth or lie? He seems so proud of himself, like he's cracked the code on how to make Papi forget his failures. The struggle for him is real. Being the only son comes with a set of unrealistic pressures that even I can't comprehend. He's named after Papi, no less. His role as the only boy in the house has been set since the beginning but I don't think Junior was ever asked whether he wanted the responsibility or not. He seeks ways to make himself out to be a big player but none of that will matter if Jasmine is pregnant with his child. Junior will have to step up to take care of that mess.

"So?" He waits.

"I think it's important that you talk to Jasmine," I say.

"For once, can you be on my side?" he says. "Is that too much to ask? Fuck. Forget you."

In spite of my lack of approval, Junior still feels compelled to walk to Papi's office. Junior doesn't have time to be a father, not when he's still trying to chase some empire dream. And what about Jasmine's dream to be a singer? Is that pushed aside because of a baby?

I hope Jasmine is mistaken.

I'm too young to be an aunt.

CHAPTER 14

scan the crowd. It's as if the artsy Latino set coordinated their calendars to come out this Saturday. The DIY girls with their multidyed hair and crazy loud outfits. The emo boys in black with their skateboards. My conservative floral dress doesn't leave any type of mark with this group. Elizabeth fits right in with her kaleidoscope jumper and black creepers.

"What do you think?" Elizabeth asks as she looks for the perfect place to set up our picnic. "A little shade, a little sun?"

"It doesn't matter."

"Hey, what about here?" She happily lays a blanket and claims a spot under a tree.

I'm still freaked out about Junior and Jasmine. I started to tell Elizabeth about the situation but she kind of brushed it off. She said I needed time away from family and their drama. Time just to have fun. So I dropped it.

"Don't be so grumpy," Elizabeth says. "The music is going to be popping."

She pulls out her phone and takes a picture of me, grumpy face and all.

"Ha. I'm so going to post this," she says.

That's not happening. I won't allow that picture to be seen by Serena and Camille. There will be no evidence of me here. I tell her to delete it.

"I'm not doing that. Stop trying to censor me," she says. "This is life and I'm documenting it. I'm thinking of doing a photo-collage for my next project."

"Do not post that because if you do I'm leaving," I say.

Elizabeth takes another picture.

"Stop taking pictures!" I say. "I'm serious."

She finally puts her phone down and studies me. She shakes her head like a mother to a child.

"You used to be fun. You are so worried about what others think."

"I'm still fun," I protest. "This just isn't my—"

Someone calls out her name.

"Elizabeth!"

The girl has a shaved head and wears a long skirt with a cropped top. Her wrists are weighted down with jewelry— silver, gold, leather. It's the total music festival uniform, a Latina hippie.

"I'm so glad you came!" she says, and hugs Elizabeth.

Without so much as a warning, she gives me a hug too.

"Hi. So nice to finally meet you," she says. "I'm Paloma. Elizabeth has told me so much about you."

Elizabeth makes room for her friend. I'm forced to meet the girl who replaced me in Elizabeth's life. The one I've been jealous about. Paloma pulls a loaf of bread and green grapes out of her tote bag, her contribution to our picnic.

"Elizabeth has been trying to connect me with you for so long," Paloma says. "I forgot. What school do you go to?"

"Margot goes to Somerset," Elizabeth answers. There's a bit of an attitude in the way she says this. Maybe I'm on edge but it sounds as if Elizabeth just threw shade.

"Yes!" Paloma says. "I heard the guys at Somerset are hot. Is that true? Because if it is I'm going to register right now."

I can see why Elizabeth likes Paloma. She looks like a human art project, with her missing hair and henna along her arms and legs. When she talks, she sounds like a musical instrument, with her bracelets jangling around.

"Have you seen Boogaloo before? Whenever they're in town, I'm front and center," Paloma says.

Before I can even answer, she stands up and flails her arms.

"That's Mimi, right? Mimi! Over here." She screams for the mysterious Mimi until she realizes it isn't her. "Oops.

But wait, that's Freddie. I'll be right back." She heads over to a large circle of guys.

"Paloma's kind of nuts," Elizabeth says. "But she's very sweet."

"Yeah, I can see that," I say. "I didn't know we were meeting your friends."

"It wasn't planned. You don't mind, do you?"

It's only been a few minutes and I already feel uncomfortable around Paloma. She hasn't said anything but I can't help but feel like the odd girl, just from appearance alone. Why couldn't this outing be just between Elizabeth and me?

I toss a couple of grapes in my mouth. Midchew, I see him. Moises stands in that circle right by Paloma. My stomach flips. I can't believe it. I'm not prepared.

"Can we go?" I get up and start packing the food.

"We just got here," Elizabeth says.

"I'm not feeling well."

Paloma leads them over to us. It's too late. I can't just up and run. He'll think I'm crazy or ashamed of what happened between us. I've got to chill.

"What's going on?" Elizabeth asks.

Moises sees me and grins. He wears a white T-shirt and worn jeans that have slight rips in them. He is so fine. I need to shake this off.

"No, nothing. Never mind." I try to compose myself. He heads our way. I can handle this. It's no big deal.

"Hey," Moises says.

"Hey," I say.

"You guys know each other!" Paloma's excitement grates on me. I wish she would tone down everything. Elizabeth elbows me but I keep my cool.

"Yeah, we go way back," Moises teases. "Never pictured you a Boogaloo lover. Can't seem to figure you out."

"Well, you're not the only one with eclectic musical tastes." I smile despite myself.

"Margot's not a fan. I am." Elizabeth reaches her hand out and introduces herself to Moises. This is a first. She's never been so bold when it comes to guys. Is this because Paloma is here? Maybe Elizabeth feels fearless with her new friend.

Moises introduces us to his friends. I recognize a couple of them from the pictures hanging on his bedroom mirror. Freddie works with Moises at the South Bronx Family Mission. Willie I met before. He works at the community garden. He's the oldest of the bunch but he doesn't talk much. They're all a little rough around the edges, like him. Paloma knows Moises from elementary school. Small world. Too small.

"How do you know each other?" Elizabeth asks. She's trying to figure out if this is the same guy I was with that night.

To smooth Elizabeth's confused state, I explain: "Moises mans a table by the supermarket."

"The supermarket?" Paloma asks.

"Margot's family owns the Sanchez & Sons supermarket by Third Avenue," Elizabeth explains to Paloma.

"Oh! Your family owns that?" Paloma exclaims. "My mom shops there every day. Your family practically feeds us."

Paloma goes on about how the supermarket was part of her childhood. No one else seems fazed by this except for me. I feel weird. I don't want to be connected to the supermarket, for that to dictate how they see me.

"You mean the one across from St. Mary's Park?" Freddie asks. "I go there all the time, bro. I know everybody. My boy Dominic works there. So does Papo but he goes by the name of P-Nice. You know 'em?"

I do but I only talk to Dominic and that's barely.

"What about the fine sisters Wanda and Lourdes?" he asks. "They still work there? Them girls are like . . . damn." He closes his eyes and bites his bottom lip. Paloma playfully hits him with her tote bag.

"What do you do there?" Elizabeth asks Moises.

"I collect signatures to stop the Eagle Avenue tenant building from being torn down to make room for condos," Moises says. He leans in to me and takes some grapes.

"Rich white people," Freddie says.

"The owners of that building aren't white," I say. The group goes quiet.

"The Carrillos haven't lived in that neighborhood for

ages," Moises says. "They've lost touch with their own people."

"Yeah, they might as well be white," Freddie says.

I roll my eyes. Why doesn't Elizabeth chime in? She could at least try to back me up.

"This is about business. And stop generalizing about groups of people. Not all white people are bad," I say. It's hard to express myself when I'm used to following Serena and Camille's leads. I also hear Papi's voice in my head, how a condo helps everyone. Helps us. He can't be wrong.

"Yeah, I'm half white." Paloma pushes Freddie. "What does that make me?"

"Beautiful." Freddie jumps on Paloma, who squeals in protest.

"Business is business," Moises says. "But looking out for those who can't speak for themselves is everyone's business."

"My father's supermarket has been there for years so he's seen the neighborhood go through many changes." I shouldn't feel bad for defending my family's stance but I do. This uneasiness is hard to brush off. "This is just one more thing."

"Where did you buy that cup of coffee you're drinking? Starbucks, right?" Yes. Elizabeth goes in after Freddie. "What existed in that place before Starbucks? I bet you it was a mom-and-pop store."

"Yeah," Paloma says. "Hypocrite."

Moises glares at Freddie until Freddie trashes his Starbucks drink.

"Damn, bro," Freddie says. "Thanks for ruining my latte swag."

"Not all change is good," Moises says. He hands Freddie a bottle of water. "If everyone has that same mentality you might as well give up and let the corporations win. What if Whole Foods opened up right by your family's supermarket? What then?"

I can see the domino effect if that were to happen. I complain about working there but the supermarket is my family's livelihood. How do you move forward without crushing others around you? I've never thought about how a new store can ruin another person's life. Our supermarkets are a fixture in the community but what if the community becomes unrecognizable? There are no easy answers. The longer I listen to Moises the more I see that not everything is painted black-and-white the way my father tells me.

A friend interrupts the conversation and the topic is dropped.

While we wait for the band to start, friends from the neighborhood stop by to say hello and to give the rundown of where others sit and what they plan to do afterwards. Moises knows them and it's like he's the top dog of this squad. They gravitate around him and listen to his every word. He is so confident. They all are, each in their own way.

Someone in the group asks him why he wasn't at the demonstration against police brutality the other night.

162

"I was busy," he says. He stares at me and my face burns up. We never agreed on the terms but he must know that what went down that night is not open for discussion. The guys goof on Moises and ask for the girl's name but he doesn't tell. I pop more grapes in my mouth.

Freddie lights up a joint and passes it around. Moises takes a long hit.

"Where did you get this shit from? Washington Square? This is oregano, papa. Don't hold out on the good shit, motherfucker." Moises's curses are jarring to hear. This is how he is with his friends. This is where he's the most comfortable. When he passes the joint over to Elizabeth, I expect her to say no but she doesn't. Elizabeth inhales as if she's smoked weed for years. I'm the only one who doesn't take a hit. In this crowd, I'm the weirdo.

There are too many people. I don't pull my conversational weight. Everyone is an artist or a poet. I'm just the girl who goes to Somerset whose father owns the supermarket. Even Elizabeth gets more play from the guys, including Moises, who is interested in her art. She shares photos of her latest work with him. Moises states how many times he's seen the Boogaloo perform. Elizabeth has their rare live tracks that only true hard-core fans know about. It's hard to watch them.

"Are you okay?" Moises nudges me after a lull in the conversation.

"I'm good."

We're barely friends. I'm fine if he speaks to Elizabeth. They seem to hit it off. He doesn't seem intent on educating her on bad corporations and poetry.

"This is *the* song!" Paloma yells. "Come dance with me."

She tries to convince Freddie to get up but he wants to smoke. The others aren't interested, including Elizabeth, who seems content talking to Moises. Paloma looks at me.

"C'mon." She takes my hand and drags me toward the stage. I don't want to dance but I'd rather do that than watch Moises and Elizabeth. Paloma pushes her way to the front of the stage and carves out a space for us. I stand behind her.

The song is a slow reggaeton and Paloma gyrates to the beat without any qualm or sense that people are staring. Men watch in awe until one brave soul ventures into her space and starts to freak her from behind. She doesn't acknowledge the boy. I keep to my safe but boring two-step dance: one step to the left, one to the right. There's nothing suggestive or sexy in the way I move. Sure, I bust out in my bedroom when I'm alone, but at school parties, I watch from the sidelines until Serena eventually drags me out for a pity dance. This could be what Paloma did. A pity dance.

I'm jealous of how she can shut out what's around her and enjoy the music. I'm aware of everything. My clumsy moves. How Moises gets along with Elizabeth. I should be happy. They make total sense but I can't shake off his kiss.

An older man with a large nose and a bandana wrapped around his head touches my arm. I tell him no. He tries again, totally not understanding that I don't want to dance with him. He starts to force the issue but Moises appears and puts his arm around my waist. He pulls me toward him. The jilted man gets the hint and walks.

"How are you gonna dance with that guy?" Moises asks.

Before I can defend myself, Moises places my arm around his neck. His knee presses in between my legs. Both our arms glisten with sweat. With his help, I finally find the right groove. I let the steady rhythmic beat of the bass and Moises guide me. I search for Elizabeth but she's nowhere to be found. I don't want her to think I'm cutting into her new man. This is only a dance.

"If you wanted to see me so badly," Moises says, "you could have told me."

"What? I didn't plan this."

"It's okay, relax," he says. "You don't have to keep your true feelings to yourself."

He laughs but it's not funny. I didn't orchestrate this meeting. It's a coincidence. I don't want any misunderstandings. There's nothing between us, even though he grinds into me and I smell his deep musk oil.

"Your friend is cool. Elizabeth, right?" he continues. "We should hang out together. Check out other concerts."

His mouth is so close to my ear. I'm glad he's interested in her. I won't let this tinge of jealousy bother me. I'm going to bury it deep because Elizabeth and Moises is a good thing.

"We don't need to hang out," I say. "Elizabeth will be more than happy to go with you to concerts."

His hand drops. What is wrong with me? I can be so cold but I can't let my emotions show, especially when they don't make sense. I want Elizabeth to get to know Moises. I do.

"Cool. Then you don't mind if I call her," he says. "We're good."

He walks away. I force myself to dance alone until the song finishes.

When I walk back to the group, Moises is sitting by Elizabeth. And although Elizabeth is not talking directly to him, I'm still upset at the seating dynamics. I sit next to Freddie.

"Can I have some?" Freddie passes the joint to me and I take the smallest hit from it. I don't even like it but I can be like the rest of them. Moises pays me no mind. None. I check my phone and leave a comment on a picture of Nick on the beach. Nothing too obvious or desperate, just a couple of swimming emojis. I scroll for another image and see a picture of Serena and Camille hanging out with Nick and friends. More than ever I wish I were there with them.

"That girl is fine." Freddie grabs my phone and ogles the picture of Serena. "Hook a brother up."

"I don't think so," I say.

Elizabeth chimes in. "She goes to Somerset. She might be out of your league."

Again, there's that tone. Even if it's true, why does she bring it up?

"Once I give off my papi chulo swag, that girl will be cooking me chuletas in no time," he says. "Pass me her number."

I grab the phone from him.

"The only thing that girl is going to do is call Five-O," Moises says. "Them girls don't want to have anything to do with you or me. Am I right?"

Moises looks at me with an expression full of accusations. I'm done with this scene.

"I'm going," I say.

"Why?" Elizabeth jumps up. She's genuinely hurt but I don't want to be here, not while Moises hates on me. She starts to pick up her stuff but she doesn't have to go.

"No. Stay," I tell her. "Have fun."

"Are you sure? You don't mind?"

"I'm positive. Call me later."

I say good-bye to everyone, except Moises. I ignore him.

CHAPTER 15

My curves bulge out. Too many Cuban sandwiches. I'll never look good enough for the Hamptons, not at this rate anyway. Countdown to the party. Only two more weeks. So far I've made about seventeen hundred dollars, which is a lot but I have seen absolutely none of it. Every cent Papi has gladly taken and he still refuses to give me some of it to buy a dress for a party that he hasn't completely committed to.

I'm heading toward aisle four, where Dominic is, when my phone buzzes with a text from Camille to urgently call her.

"Nick asked for you," Camille says when she answers the phone. "He needs to speak to you. Can you talk?"

"Why does he want to speak to me?"

"Shut up. Just get ready. He's calling you," Camille says. She practically pants on the phone. This is some craziness.

"And Margot, it's on FaceTime so you better look good."

"But why? What does he want?"

Camille breathes heavily into the phone. She is irked. "He wants to ask you something. When he calls, let it ring three times, then answer it."

She hangs up without saying good-bye. Shit. I'm not ready for whatever this is. I run to the bathroom and take a quick inventory. I didn't blow out my hair. The curls spill out. I have no eye makeup. I put on lipstick and pinch my cheeks. My hands are already sweating. Maybe he's going to ask me out. The girls probably chatted him up and he's decided that the time is right for us. Finally, something good is about to happen. I can stop obsessing over Moises and Elizabeth with Nick on my line.

Waiting is hard. I look at the phone to make sure it's on. Reapply lipstick. Fix my hair.

"Hey, are you going to help me or what?" Dominic asks as he replenishes the boxes of pasta. I take one box and place it on the shelf.

"I am helping." I check the phone again.

When it rings, I run outside. Daylight will be a better look than artificial indoor lighting. One ring. Two rings. On the third ring, I pick up. Nick appears fuzzy on the tiny screen.

"Hi, Margot?" he says. There's a slight delay so when he says something, it doesn't quite sync.

"Hi, Nick." The sound of an ambulance siren screeches by. "Can you hear me? I'm outside so it might be noisy. Sorry about that."

"No problem. How's your summer?" He's calling from inside a room. His bedroom? Even though his hair is long and messy he looks good in a blue shirt. My heart races and I try my best not to talk over him or fiddle with my charm necklace. Composure. Be still.

"My summer's been amazing. And you? I mean, and yours?" I try to confine my answers to one or two syllables.

"Good. Haven't seen you at the beach. What's up with that?"

He's been looking for me.

"Been working," I say.

"Hope it hasn't been all work."

My cackle of a laugh hurts my own ears. Pull it together. There's a pause and I'm not sure if it's the connection or if I should say something.

"Playing soccer?" I ask, and immediately regret it. What a stupid question. Who cares? I sound like an idiot.

"Sometimes."

Another siren passes and I apologize again. I'm so embarrassed.

"So, Serena and Camille told me you have some sort of supermarket connection."

"Oh." My face drops. What did they say? I'm scared of

what he must think of me. A supermarket connection. What does that even mean? It sounds ridiculous.

"Yeah, we're throwing the party and I thought maybe . . . You're definitely coming. Right?"

"Yes, I'm definitely going to be there." He wants me there!

"I was thinking." He looks away from the phone as if he's shy. It's cute. "Since you have a supermarket connection you might be able to get us a deal on some beer."

"Beer?" I repeat. He wants me to score him some beer. How random. And why would he be worried about money? I thought his father was some boss at a tech company.

"My father is cracking down on me this summer. You know how it is." He leaves it at that and I nod. It surprises me to hear that he has to deal with money problems. They're probably cutting down his allowance from a whole lot to just a lot.

"Just thought I would ask," he says. "But if you can't it's not a big deal. I can figure something out."

"No, no. I can totally help," I say. "I would love to."

How am I supposed to get beer? Sure, my parents own a supermarket but things are really tight. I wouldn't be able to ask them. Not only that, I'm a minor. Just because my parents own a store doesn't mean I can take whatever I want. I can't even grab a pack of M&M's without being forced to pay. I share none of this.

"Great," Nick says. "We just need about three cases. Let me know how you want to handle it."

"Sure, I can send you a text or something."

"The party is going to be epic," Nick says. "Can't wait."

"Me too." And we smile at each other.

Papi storms out of the supermarket and into the parking lot. His face is red. Junior follows close behind.

"Enough already!" Papi yells at Junior.

I try to find a quieter area but the blare of a car horn adds to the confusion.

"You know these guys. I introduced you to them!" Junior yells to Papi. There's a tinge of panic in his voice. "Let's take a drive over there right now so I can show you."

"What I need from you is to focus on the supermarket instead of wasting my time with your maldita bar idea!" screams Papi.

"Is everything okay?" Nick asks. "Where are you?"

"Yes, everything is fine," I say as I duck into a corner and try to keep Nick from witnessing the family drama unfolding in public. "Just some random crazy people."

"Let me crunch the numbers for you. I know this bar would be a good investment," Junior says.

"You can't even crunch the supermarket numbers," Papi says. "What makes you think I'll trust you with some bar?"

"This is about the supermarket," Junior says. " I'm trying to help. Can't you see that? Let me do this for the family."

Papi shakes his head. He is not giving in even with Junior begging.

"As usual, you don't trust me. When are you going to stop treating me like a boy? I'm going to get that fucking money," Junior says. "With or without you!"

"Sorry," I say to Nick. My ears burn up from shame. "I'll text you when I have details."

"Can't wait to see you," Nick says. He hangs up while Papi and Junior continue their war. To avoid the insanity, I race back inside.

If this plan works, Nick will see me as someone worthy of spending time with. I'll come back to Somerset with an amazing story, an angle, of how I saved the summer. For once, working at a supermarket will be an asset. I have to figure it out. There's so much to do.

When it's time to go home, I head up to Papi's office. He smiles at me and I take that as a good sign that maybe he isn't still fuming from his argument with Junior.

"I'm glad you're here," he says. "I have to stay late today. Junior will take you home."

Great. I have to ride with that anger. Junior will probably crash the car. But I can't complain about that. There are pressing matters I must attend to right now, namely the party.

"Papi, I've been working hard," I say as sweetly as

possible. "Can I go to my friend's party next week in the Hamptons? Summer is almost over and I haven't done much of anything."

"What party?" He returns to his work. "What did your mother say?"

Thank god Mami is on board. This is easier than I thought.

"She said it was up to you." He's going to say yes, I can feel it.

"Fine."

Now for the real ask.

"Thank you!" I say. "And Papi, can I also have money so I can buy something to wear?"

He massages his forehead.

"You kids haven't learned anything. I am not a bank!" His face is red from anger. "No, you can't have money for a dress. Clothes are what got you in trouble in the first place. The answer is no."

This was a huge mistake. I aimed too high. I need to back down before he reneges on the party. One thing at a time. First I need permission to go. Then I can figure out how I'm going to secure some beers.

"Sorry, Papi." I leave his office before he starts yelling at me like he yelled at Junior.

I find my brother by his locker, shirtless. What used to be his pride and joy, his ridged stomach, is now nothing but protruding ribs. He's lost some serious weight. Something is eating him up badly and I think I know what it is. Stress.

"You need to drive me home," I say.

Junior ignores me. He puts on one of his bedazzled T-shirts and splashes cologne on his neck.

"Did you hear me?" I ask. "You owe me. You told that lie to Papi about me and Moises. You know I'm not talking to him."

There's no reaction from Junior.

"It's a lie and you know it."

"I'm protecting you," he mumbles. "I know about Moises."

"I know some things too. I heard you and his brother Orlando used to be tight," I say. "But you don't see me spilling that bit of information to Papi, do you? Or that crazy situation with Jasmine."

There's a slight flinch. He didn't expect that from me. Maybe he'll back off and give me some space.

"What situation with Jasmine?" The way he asks gives me the impression that he doesn't have a clue. What if it's not him? I don't want to be the person to break the news.

"You should talk to Jasmine," I say. "Really."

"I'm not talking to Jasmine. My only concern is my baby sister," Junior says. His voice is raspy. "There are things you shouldn't be worrying about."

Right. I've heard that sentence so many times it's

imprinted in my skin. Everyone in this family is so hush-hush about the scary things in the world. All the blindfolding isn't helping.

"I'm not seeing Moises," I say. "I swear."

"I believe you." Junior's voice is still a grunt but there's a hint of gentleness in there that I recognize. The Junior I remember is buried deep somewhere. The brother who rushed over to me when I tripped on that rock in Hawaii and scraped my knee. He picked me up and held my hand while I got stitches. It's the same brother who keeps a picture of us taken at my First Holy Communion ceremony by his bedside table.

"Are you ready?" he says. I nod and follow him to his car.

Although Junior drives, he can't stop checking his phone. It rings and rings. His answers are very cryptic. From what I gather, he needs to meet a guy to give him something later tonight.

"What's going on with the missing money?" I ask. "Has it stopped?"

"What do you know about that?" He speaks sharply. Well, that's my answer right there. Someone steals and we have no idea who. How hard can it be to figure out?

"Everyone at the store knows. Shouldn't we be getting the cops involved?"

"Naw. I got my suspicion of who it is. I just need proof,"

he says. "We'll handle it in-house. Don't worry about it."

I watch the people do the rush-hour stampede. On a mission. Our family is on a mission too, to keep serious issues on lockdown. When I asked why Junior got kicked out of school, my parents refused to give me a straight answer. Instead, I found out when Papi made the mistake of leaving the official probation letter on the kitchen table. After yelling at me for snooping around, Mami made me promise to keep Junior's situation a secret. Under no circumstances was I to gossip about this to anyone, not even Elizabeth. It was nobody's business and it would only hurt Junior. It took so much for me not to tell Elizabeth. The family fell behind the lie that it was Junior's decision to leave the school and not the other way around.

Soon after that I stopped sharing a lot of things with Elizabeth. I got into Somerset and I guess I was protecting myself. I didn't want her to know about the embarrassing situations I was getting into. It's the running theme in my life. My family tries to shelter me from the ugliness of the world. I've learned to ignore the bad and put up fake fronts to fool the people around me. But it's getting harder to pretend.

Junior pulls into our driveway. He locks the car door to stop me from leaving and pulls out a wad of cash from his pocket. He holds out a good chunk of fifty-dollar bills.

"What the hell, Junior? Where did you get this money?"

"Doing some club marketing for friends. I know Papi is being stingy with you. He is so fucking cheap. I'm never going to be like that. Buy yourself something nice. Okay?" he says. The bills practically spill out of his hand. "We'll find out who's stealing. Don't worry."

Hush money. Don't talk about Jasmine's situation or the stolen money. Take the cash and seal the deal. I keep being Princesa and he keeps being Junior. I shouldn't do it but I can so use the cash. It's more than enough for me to buy a cute dress.

"You know I love you, right?" Junior waits anxiously for me to take it, to erase any previous wrongdoing with a simple action. "I'm serious. This shit at the supermarket is a big fucking headache but it's not about you. Be a good sister."

I need this money so I take it. And with money in my hand, I continue the family denial. I step out of the car.

CHAPTER 16

Money is being drained out of our family's store. Everyone is nervous about losing their jobs, especially after Papi laid off a couple of the cashieristas. There's no doubt the family business is struggling this summer. What should be our busiest season draws to an end with a whimper instead of a bang. I know this. It still doesn't stop me from going ahead with my plan. Papi and Junior are scheduled to visit the second location, like they do every Friday. Junior never wants to go but he really has no choice. I worked it all out. I have to secure the beers. I won't call it stealing. It's a contribution to the Margot Social Fund.

This weekend is the only time when I can finally have a little bit of fun. I'm going to show up and Nick and everyone else from Somerset will see that the girl who came in completely clueless can hold her own.

This is what I tell myself as I pretend to work alongside Dominic.

"Then my girl wanted to go to Orchard Beach but I'm not trying to hit that beach," Dominic says. "Too many peckerheads trying to sabotage my game."

I twirl my necklace and ignore the mark it leaves on my neck from my intense twist. My eyes follow Papi as he gathers his stuff. They have to leave soon or my plan won't work.

"So, do you think my girl had a reason for getting mad at me?" Dominic asks.

"What? No, I mean, I don't know. Please shut up. I'm trying to think."

Papi walks down from his office. He makes small talk with the customers and then goes over something with Oscar. He almost changed his mind about letting me to go to the party. He said I had to keep Mami company because he was going to be tied up at work this weekend. Mami doesn't want me around. She's like a ghost. There but not really there. Mami's depressed about something and won't share the reason why with me. She spends most of her time watching television or talking on the phone with her sisters back in Puerto Rico.

Papi wouldn't relent until Mami got involved. The discussion soon shifted into how Junior wastes time on outside projects instead of the supermarket. They both started to argue and soon enough my trip to the Hamptons was back on. I laid the groundwork earlier in the week by alerting everyone that I would leave early today.

No one knows about this plan. Not Elizabeth, whom I haven't spoken to since that time at the park. Serena and Camille only care that I get the cases of beer and look cute.

I get a text from Nick letting me know that his cousin is about a half hour away from the supermarket. Thankfully Papi and Junior are almost out the door. I wait until I'm sure they've driven out of the parking lot. Then I wait an extra ten minutes for good measure.

"Dominic, I've got to take care of some things before I head out," I say.

I grab a shopping cart and make a note of where Oscar is positioned. He's in the main office, which overlooks the row of registers. Like on any regular day, I greet the customers. They smile back. Roberto gives me the side-eye as I push the cart past the deli section. There's nothing out of the ordinary going on over here. Just Princesa doing some shopping. My heart rate increases as I push the cart toward where the back inventory is kept. In my hand, I hold the list of preferred beer brands. This has been worked out with Nick. He wanted to buy cheap beer but I convinced him he should at least buy some imported ones. Like I knew what I was talking about. I don't even drink but I am the girl with the supermarket connection. Nick got his cousin to drive to the Bronx to pick me up. My parents think I'm catching a ride with Serena's parents. They didn't even bother checking if any of what I said was true. When Nick offered to send me money, I told him not to bother. Nick said he couldn't wait to see me. I replayed these phone conversations over and over in my head. It's easy to forget about Moises when I do that.

The other workers are too busy with their day to pay any attention to me. Jasmine is not around. She called in sick, which she's been doing a lot lately. I'm guessing morning sickness. But I don't want to think about her or her drama. I'm only thinking about the Hamptons.

The first case is a little heavy but I place it carefully on the shopping cart. I scan the area again. The coast is still clear. I start to lift the second case.

"Yo, what's up? It's me, you know, from Boogaloo Bad Boys."

Moises's friend Freddie is standing in front of me with a big bag of potato chips in his hand. Freddie looks at the case of beer and then at me.

"Where's the party?" he says.

"There's no party," I say. "You shouldn't be back here."

Without me asking, he helps lift the second case and places it in the cart.

"I was just hanging with Papo, you know, P-Nice. Anyway, it looks like a party to me, unless you have a serious drinking problem. Then what I got to say to you about that is get some help."

He refuses to leave my side even when I push the shopping cart to find more beer.

"It's just a small get-together with some friends," I say. "Okay, I got to go. Bye."

"The girl in the picture is going to be there?" Freddie will not stop and he won't leave.

"Maybe. I don't know." Can't he take a hint? I send him a full range of signals: I don't make eye contact. Two-to-three-word sentences for answers. I practically give him my back. Nothing. He eats out of the now-opened bag of potato chips, completely clueless.

"You should go pay for that," I say. "There's always a line. Also, customers are not allowed here. You need to leave. It was good seeing you."

"I got no plans tonight," he says. "What's popping with you and your friends?"

I didn't ask him about his plans. Freddie's fishing for an invite. I can't deal with him right now. Please go away.

"Princesa."

Damn it. Oscar calls to me.

"What are you doing?" he asks. I'm so busted.

"I'm just grabbing some supplies," I quickly say.

Oscar places a hand on the shopping cart. This is failing

and I can see how it will go down. Serena and Camille will write me off for my lack of initiative. Nick won't even know what happened because I will continue to be a nothing. A big void.

"You can't take those," Oscar says. He turns to Freddie. "Who are you?"

Freddie raises his eyebrows and takes a step back like he's trying to walk away from the scene of the crime. I give him a pleading look. He doesn't owe me a thing but whether he likes it or not, he's now mixed up in my plan.

"I already rang them up." I show Oscar the receipt I fudged earlier that morning. He doesn't budge.

"Who is this for?" Oscar grabs the shopping cart and pulls it away from me. Not even tears will sway him. This foolish mission is falling apart.

"They're for this nonprofit organization. It's a fundraiser to help raise money for summer equipment for homeless kids. Right, Freddie?" The lies flow out of me like water. Freddie's eyes are wide but he keeps his mouth shut.

"Sorry, Princesa, but I can't have funny business going on today," Oscar says.

"No, you don't understand," I say. "I took care of it already. Papi said it was fine."

"Un fundraiser?" Oscar asks suspiciously. He rubs the back of his bald head.

Oscar has to believe me. He loves me. My phone buzzes. It must be my ride.

"And your father knows?" he says with uncertainty.

Another long pause. Freddie eats the potato chips. He waits to see how this will pan out. At least he's not ratting me out or making things worse by talking.

"Bueno. Next time you have to talk to me first. There's a process we have to go through when it comes to alcohol. Me entiendes?"

"Yes. Sorry, Oscar," I say. "I thought since Papi said it was fine, I didn't need to bother you. You seemed so busy."

"I'm never busy for you. We're family." His face is crestfallen and I can tell he's disappointed. We both know I'm lying but he's going to let me get away with it anyway. "Espero que sepas lo que haces." I hope you know what you're doing, he says. I can't even look him in the eye but I still keep the syrupy grin plastered on my face. No matter what, I will stick to this fabricated story even at the cost of Oscar losing respect for his Princesa. If he rats me out to my father, by the time he does I'll be by the beach and it will be too late.

"Gracias," I say.

Someone calls Oscar's name.

"They need you out front."

Oscar hesitates for a few seconds more but soon he leaves to tend to another crisis.

"Okay." Freddie elongates the word for emphasis. "I'm confused. First off: Who the hell is Princesa?"

"Princesa is my nickname." I answer the text and push the cart. "Sorry, I didn't mean to put you in a bind. The situation was kind of out of my hands."

"Uh-huh." He walks with me to the parking lot. I search for a blue BMW. A guy in shorts waves at me. That must be Nick's cousin. There's a slight resemblance. He has the same kind of build, that same easygoing attitude.

"You must be Margot," he says. "I'm Chris."

He shakes my hand and introduces himself to Freddie, who still refuses to leave my side. Chris opens the trunk and Freddie helps lift a case.

"Hey, Chris, what time is the party?" Freddie asks.

I don't acknowledge the question.

"Not sure," Chris says. "I'm just the courier service."

"So probably around eight p.m., right?" Freddie asks.

"He's kidding. No, you are not invited," I say, and laugh nervously. "Thanks for helping me, though."

"I hooked you up, Princesa slash Margot," Freddie says. "C'mon."

My palms sweat. Chris glances at his watch. I set down the last case and he closes the trunk.

"I'll be right back," I say. "I just need to get my bag."

"Cool. We should head out soon," Chris says. "Don't want to get caught up in that Friday traffic."

I nod and walk as fast as I can. Freddie is right at my heels.

"You can't come," I say to him.

"Then I'm going to have to talk to Oscar and tell him the organizers for the fundraiser to help save homeless kids with new baseball bats will have to buy their beer elsewhere."

This creep is blackmailing me. Freddie is not going to the party. I don't even think he owns a car. I can make up an address. No, I can't. He lives near here. He says he's always at the supermarket. And who knows? He could totally tell on me.

"Listen, Freddie. It's not going to be fun," I say. "You won't know anyone and you probably won't like the people."

"Damn. You think I ain't got no play?" Freddie says. "I go to Bronx High School of Science. I can speak on some chemical level if I have to. Physics. Advanced algebra."

"Sorry. It's a private party."

"Moises told me you were a bit on the bougie side but I didn't believe him. Your girl Elizabeth is down-to-earth. But I'm feeling some serious Latina resistance from you," he says. "I'm sure your crew can hang. It's not like they're drinking Courvoisier. What you got there? Heinies?"

Moises talks about me. Why? They probably had a laugh that day at the park. How I'm a conceited princess with stuck-up friends.

"I'm not bougie and neither are my friends."

"Why are you trying to come between me and that fine friend of yours? Text me the address, though. Here's my number."

The guy will not let up. It's not like Serena would ever speak to Freddie. She likes basketball players and Freddie's gut tells me he's on some cuchifrito diet. Oscar peers into the parking lot. Maybe he's about to change his mind. I need to finish this transaction.

"Fine. Here." I give Freddie the address. He's not going to show up so there's nothing to worry about.

"I'm definitely going to try to make it," he says. "But there's the whole transportation thing. The Hamptons is far."

When he asks for a ride, I respond with a scary face.

"I might see you tonight." He finishes up the bag of potato chips. "It's a big maybe. If I can find a ride . . ."

I'm not stressing it. There's no way Freddie is going. He's like Moises—all talk. Whatever. I've got to focus. My big entrance is on its way. It will work.

I got the beers! See you soon, I text Serena and Camille. I'm set. Nothing will ruin my moment.

CHAPTER 17

Chris stops the car in front of the gate and punches a code to open it. My mouth drops. The beach house is massive. There are large windows everywhere, a sure sign that Nick's family has nothing to hide. The slow crawl over the gravel driveway is long enough to complete my freak-out.

"Here you go," Chris says as he parks in front of the house. We didn't hit much traffic so the ride in was a lot quicker than I thought it would be. I was nervous. I didn't want to sound like an idiot in case it would get back to Nick so I kept quiet for the most part. Chris is finishing up his MBA at NYU. He lives in the city with his girlfriend. He's roughly the same age as Junior. It's hard not to compare him to my brother.

Chris stacks the cases of beer over by the side of the

house. He's off to meet his girlfriend at her parents' home nearby. "Tell Nick I'll catch him later." I thank him and he drives off.

I pull a compact mirror out and take one long look at myself. My hair is blown straight. My cute outfit was laid out two days ago. No deli meat smell. Good. Still, butterflies have hijacked my stomach, I reapply my lipstick. The walk up to the door seems like miles in these heels. I scan the windows in the hope of seeing Serena and Camille. Although it's early, they promised they would be here. There's no sign of Nick either.

The front door is unlocked, another sign that I've entered a different world. I hesitate by the door. This year I've pinned my hopes on a group of people I don't know and who don't know me. It can take just one person to call me out and label me a wannabe. To look at my clothes and listen to my accent and see how much I don't know a thing about this world. This is what I've been waiting for this summer but I'm scared. What if I'm not enough?

Inside, the place is even more intense. Everything is straight out of some magazine. The furniture is modern with slick lines in grays and blues. No loud colors or family pictures on the walls. A house where people shouldn't really touch anything for fear of breaking it.

A small group of guys stand over a long dining room table. They take shots of what looks like tequila while screaming, "Shot, shot, shot!" I recognize one of them from science class. I read in one of Mami's self-help books that sometimes "you have to fake it until you make it." This is what I repeat to myself when I approach them.

"Hi, Jason," I say. "Is Nick around?"

The guys check me out. They approve and that feels good. My anxiety is still on level ten but I can cover it and try to act as casual as possible.

"He's around here somewhere," Jason says. "Take a shot."

"Maybe later." No need to jump at the first request. I have the rest of the night to impress. Besides, I'm waiting for Nick. I text the girls.

A deejay spins music at the far end of a mostly empty living room. Only a couple of people dance. I guess the deejay is waiting for more of a crowd before setting off the dance floor. I walk farther inside and say hi to a couple of familiar faces. Two girls greet me like I'm some long-lost friend with hugs and questions about where I've been. I answer with the approved script I've made up. I tell them I've been helping with my father's business. They don't even care. All they want to do is talk about their summer so I listen.

"Have you seen Serena and Camille?" I ask.

"They were here a second ago. Check by the pool."

A cool breeze sweeps through the house. The sliding doors that face the beach are wide open. I can't imagine what it must be like to live here, to have a vacation home with a large swimming pool and a view. Access to the beach whenever you want. Even though Nick tells me his parents are a little down on him when it comes to money, how strict can they be? They still let him throw this party while they're away. My parents would never allow that to happen.

"Margot!" Serena screams from the balcony. She has a large flower tucked behind her ear and a drink in her hand. I wave.

"I'm coming down!" she says.

This is the moment of truth. I take a quick scan and press down my flyaway strands of hair. I tell myself to leave my charm necklace alone. There's no reason to be nervous. I did what I set out to do. I wait for my props for a mission accomplished and to reap the rewards from it.

"Hi!" Serena hugs me tight. She smells like suntan lotion and liquor. "You're finally here! I missed you."

"I just got here. Where's Nick? I got the beer. Should we get the cases?"

Serena laughs. "Slow down. You don't want to seem desperate."

I'm thankful that she whispers this in my ear. I want to do the right thing.

"Aren't you hot in that?" she asks.

I'm wearing a pretty tame printed dress that doesn't show much skin, not like most of the girls here. I couldn't, not after the weight I've gained from eating good pizza. If she doesn't like my clothes, Camille will definitely give it a no. I feel like a fashion failure. I undo another button and try to show what little cleavage I have.

"You have a lot of catching up to do," Serena says. She hands me her drink and I take a sip. It's so strong that it burns my throat but I don't cough. Serena squeezes my shoulder and leads me upstairs. She stops at certain cliques and lets people know I've arrived. It's as if I'm being presented to the group, like I'm making my debut of sorts. It feels good even when my smile seems about to shatter from its fakeness.

"Here's the lowdown: Nick stepped out to go pick somebody up," Serena says. She leans into me too much. I bet she's been drinking for a while. "Rebecca is trying her best to talk to him but she doesn't have a chance because, well, she's Rebecca and you are you."

Rebecca is a dancer with long muscular legs. Who wouldn't want to be with a girl who can touch her toes and do the splits? But Serena thinks I'm good enough.

"She better step away from my man," I say.

Serena laughs. "You might want to talk to him first before laying claim."

"I've talked to him!" She twists her mouth. I guess my short exchange around beer doesn't count. "Where's Camille?"

"Camille? Where do you think?" Serena points to the balcony. Camille is surrounded by most of the water polo team. Massive guys. She holds court like a queen. It's time to amp up what little courage I have again.

"Margot!" Camille yells, and the group turns to me. "How are you, bitch?"

Camille likes to do this thing in public where she talks hard, cursing and stuff, but it always sounds funny coming from her. In her midriff blouse, pleated miniskirt, and hair pulled back in a ponytail, she looks more like a tennis player than a rough girl. Sometimes I feel like she acts this way for my benefit, as if me being Latina means she has to outdo my uniqueness.

"You look so pale," she says after hugging me. "Aren't you supposed to be Puerto Rican? I think I'm darker than you." She presses her arm next to mine to check.

"I may be pale but at least I won't be getting skin cancer," I say. One guy laughs. Camille doesn't. I'm so used to dealing with Dominic at the supermarket that I've forgotten my role. I revert to what I'm meant to do whenever I'm around Camille—be her praising puppy.

"Oh my god, where did you get those earrings?" I touch the large diamond studs. "They're practically blinding me."

I need Camille to like me and she does when I like her more.

"A little something from Dad. Aren't they the shit?" she

says. "Cute dress. Zara, right? They make good Prada rip-offs. I should know because Mom has the original. You guys know Margot?"

Of course she would rag on my dress. But it's worth it, this tiny bit of humiliation, just for the introduction.

Camille leans in. "Did you bring the beer?"

I nod.

"Good work, bitch. You're making up for leaving us stranded," she says. "We had plans and you fucked it up."

"I didn't fuck it up. It was my parents."

"Yeah, I know. You were stuck working. Blah blah blah. Sucks for you because we've been having fun. Right, Serena?"

She doesn't have to remind me. Serena and Camille document every single moment online and like a true friend, I've liked and left comments on each image. Camille is retelling their Fourth of July party, a story I've heard already, but I listen. Her chilly reception will change. It takes time for her to warm up. Maybe more compliments will help. I feel rusty around them.

The guys stare at her and I'm once again invisible. It's a familiar feeling. I hate it. I don't want this to be my life. So I grab a beer off the hand of one of the water polo players and chug it down.

"Hey!" he says.

His buddies cheer me on. Camille approves because this is also what I'm good for—entertainment.

"See, I'm making up for lost time," I say. The beer is nasty but I endure it.

Serena shakes her head. "Oh, Margot! Always doing something." She playfully bumps into me.

"This bitch is taking care of you so you better bow down," Camille says. "If it weren't for Margot, you dorks would still be drinking this cheap garbage."

Camille wraps her arm around mine and I know I'm in.

"Here." She hands the guy with the missing beer her phone. "Take a picture of us."

Camille places herself in the middle, Serena to her right and me to her left. I cross my legs and tilt my head the way Camille taught me to do. Finally, a summer photo that documents the life I want.

"I love you guys so much," Serena slurs.

"You're drunk already," I say to her.

"And? Get drunk too!" she yells. I gently push her. She lands on a guy's lap and laughs uncontrollably.

Someone covers my eyes. I turn to curse the person out and find Nick grinning back at me. Nick. He looks good. Tanned. Taller, even. This is the prize I've dreamt of for so long, for Nick to finally take notice, and here he is. My tongue feels heavy.

"Been looking for you," he says. "Thanks again for the cases. You didn't have to do that but I'm glad you did. And I'm glad you're here."

"You want to go get them?" I say. "The stacks are right outside."

"No rush," he says. "We will in a second."

He has an eager look. So does everyone else. The notebook I carry in my purse conceals a list I made titled "Conversation Starters." Full-fledged encounters with Nick, drawn out on paper. I studied them. Now that he's in front of me I can't think of a single thing to say that will make me sound witty or even human.

"Doesn't Margot look great?" Serena says. I know she means well but I can't help but feel foolish. It's the same feeling I get when Papi puts me on display with the customers like I'm some limited-edition doll.

"We should go," I say. Anything to move away from these prying eyes. "I don't want the beers to get hot."

"Sure, no problem," Nick says. "Let's go."

"Wait a sec," Camille says. The girls surround me. Serena pulls lint off my dress. Then Camille whispers in my ear, "Dance with him."

They both look at me like I'm about to walk the runway or accept the winner's crown. I guess I did in a way win something. Nick leads me back downstairs by the crook of my arm. Like a gentleman. And because it's his house, people step aside. I don't feel invisible because I'm with him. I giggle when I see Rebecca crane her neck to catch a glimpse of us together.

"What's so funny?" he asks, squeezing my arm just a tiny bit.

"Nothing. Never mind," I say. "It's just up ahead."

For once, I'm winning the prizes. The night is just beginning.

"Yo, wassup, Princesa!"

It's unsettling to hear my nickname. No one from Somerset knows me by that name and definitely no one here in the Hamptons. I strain to look where the voice came from. With the setting sun, it's hard to tell.

"Princesa! Over here!"

Freddie leans his head out of a car. He opens the door and steps out. Willie, the guy who works at the garden next to my parents' supermarket, joins him. Seconds later, Moises exits the same car. My heart falls to the ground.

CHAPTER 18

Freddie, Moises, and Willie walk toward us. What are they doing here? This is a nightmare.

"Do you know those guys?" Nick asks.

I can't speak. What is Moises thinking? Is he here to humiliate me in front of all of Somerset?

"Hey, Princesa," Freddie says. "This place is dope."

"What are you doing here?" I don't want Nick to think anything is wrong so I temper my anger by acting surprised.

"You said it was cool to come. A shawty hooked us up with the gate code because you forgot to give it to me. We good?" Freddie asks Nick. Moises keeps quiet. His only expression? That sly smirk I know so well. I die a little inside.

"I wasn't going to make it but then, toma, Moises convinced Willie to drive his aunt's car." Freddie pats Moises's shoulder. "I'm Freddie, by the way. This is Moises and Willie."

Nick shakes Freddie's hand.

"It's definitely cool," Nick says. "I'm Nick."

"Aw, so you're Nick." Moises finally speaks. "Margot's told me all about you. Nice house."

"Thanks." Nick shakes his hand. "Are you guys related to Margot or something?"

"Naw, Margot and I . . . we're just friends."

Moises wears a grungy shirt and jeans. His sneakers are scuffed up too. If he planned to crash the party, he could have at least tried to look like he cared. Freddie and Willie look somewhat presentable but Moises looks as if he walked off a rally.

"They're friends of the family," I say.

"Great. You're welcome to stay," Nick adds. "Mi casa es su casa."

"Oh. You speak Spanish?" Moises asks. "Cool. It's probably what Margot sees in you—an appreciation of the language."

I can't do this. Moises is being a jerk and Nick can't even tell because he's a nice guy.

"I'm not that fluent, not like Margot." Nick doesn't catch Moises's sarcastic tone. "I picked up some Spanish when I was in Guatemala, building houses."

"For real?" Moises says. "Margot likes people who give back. Right, Margot?"

"I do." I watch Moises's wide grin falter as I inch closer to Nick.

"Um, okay," Nick says, a little confused. "Let's get these bad boys inside."

"We'll help you out, bro," Freddie says. He touches up his hair and smooths his shirt before grabbing a case. Nick and Willie take the other two.

"Do you mind if I check out the beach?" Moises says. "Spent the summer working. Haven't had a chance to chill by the water."

"Go right ahead," Nick says.

Moises walks away without a care. This is some kind of heartless game. Serena and Camille will recognize Moises the minute he hits the party. I can't have that. He's trying to ruin my night. There's no way I'm going to let him think I'm okay with him being here. I storm after him.

"What the hell are you doing?"

"Freddie said there was a party," Moises says. He continues to walk to the beach. "There's a deejay so it seems pretty legit. Sounds like they're playing hip-hop. Maybe I'll bust out some dance moves."

"Liar," I say. "This has nothing to do with Freddie or the party."

This is his way of making me feel bad for insulting him at the concert. I was just trying to hook him up with

Elizabeth. I've been clear with him from the beginning that I'm not into him in that way. I mean, I am, but I can't. I haven't spoken to Elizabeth since then but who knows? They're probably connecting way more than I ever will.

"What are you trying to prove?" I say. "This isn't your crowd."

He stops and faces the shore.

"I just wanted to meet the friends who got you stealing," he says.

Of course. There it is. Everything boils inside. I'm so angry. I don't want him to be my conscience. I shouldn't be made to feel guilty. Not by him.

"Fuck you, Moises. I've seen the way you live," I say. "I know your history. You're no better than me."

Moises bends down and examines broken seashells and seaweed pulled in from the ocean.

"I don't go to the beach enough," he says calmly as if my curses have barely any effect on him. "We're meant to live here, right by the water. Funny how these beaches are private. Only the lucky few can enjoy them, like your friend Nick."

I see red. Why would he go to the trouble of driving way out here just to hate on my friends? The crowd back at the party grows louder. Laughter and screams. What am I even doing here?

"This is some kind of a cruel joke," I say.

"No. I borrowed my aunt's car. She trusts me so it wasn't a big deal," he says. "There was a time when she wouldn't but that was a long time ago."

"I'm not talking about that," I say. "I'm serious, Moises."

There's a long pause. He caresses the back of his neck.

"I wanted to see you," he says. "I'm not going to lie. At first I thought it was a physical thing but it's more. And I think you feel the same way."

Although my body warms up because of what he says, I can't help but feel sad too. Sad enough that I have to look away. My friends at Somerset may not know me but I accepted that a long time ago. They like the small amounts of personality I reveal. With Moises, I expose too much and I'm unable to defend myself.

He sits down on the sand.

"That party ain't going nowhere. Just sit here with me for a sec," he says. "I promise to leave in a few. I won't ruin your night."

The waves are mesmerizing to watch but I can still make out the bass of a song. A reminder of where I should be.

"Five minutes," he adds.

What is it about Moises that compels me to stay? Eventually, I sit down. He moves closer to me, close enough that our knees touch. We sit like that for what feels like forever. There are so many mixed-up feelings. I keep my eyes glued to the ocean because he's staring at me but I can't keep it up. Soon I turn to face him.

"Let's just get out of here," Moises says. "You and me. "

He cups my face like he did that time on the roof. We kiss and it's everything. But then Nick and the rest of Somerset enter my thoughts, as do Elizabeth and Papi. I know I belong somewhere else, so I pull away.

Moises stares down at the sand. He picks up one of the seashells.

"It's true what they say about me. I used to sell drugs," he says. "It was a role everybody expected me to take, especially after Orlando got busted. But my aunt and friends showed me that I didn't have to be that person."

He blows the sand off the seashell and hands it to me.

"I know what it feels like to want to belong," he says. "You stealing those cases for your friends, that ain't you. Not the real you anyway."

His brown eyes seek to connect. He speaks in a gentle manner but his words still sting. This is my choice. I'm going to be a person people will admire. This is the role I choose to take.

"I don't know what you're talking about."

I drop the seashell, stand up, and walk away from him. The party is straight ahead. I walk in the direction of the other life that waits for me. I don't know if Moises is following me. I don't look back.

My first task is to take a shot of something strong because I don't know how else to deal. The second is to find Nick. A shot is easy. In fact, I take two. I locate Nick in the kitchen with Rebecca.

"Hi, Nick." I cut right in front of Rebecca like she doesn't even exist. I stake my claim. "Been looking for you. Come dance with me."

The shots take over and give me courage. Nick doesn't seem to notice. And why should he? He's never really heard me speak before.

In the corner of my eye, Moises watches this go down.

A person pushes into me. The kitchen is hot with people grabbing beers from the cases I've provided. This should make me happy, but instead I feel as if the walls are closing in. To keep me from getting trampled, Nick leads me to a window. I close my eyes and relish the breeze that comes in from the beach.

"You look pretty tonight," Nick says. His hand glides to my waist and lands softly against my back. I keep my eyes closed. Nick leans in closer and I smell his strong cologne. He smells expensive. The room spins and the only thing keeping me from landing on my face is my grip on the windowsill.

The deejay plays the latest from rapper MiT and everyone hollers. I'm swept up as we run to the living room. I spot Freddie and Willie. They sit on a sofa by a couple of girls. Freddie is saying something. The girls are laughing at him, with him? I don't know. Freddie looks at me and gives me a nod. He seems right at home here. How does that even work, to feel comfortable no matter the circumstances? Moises gives Freddie and Willie the pound, then walks across the room.

Why can't this be easy for me? My dance moves are clumsy. After a while, I just press against Nick. He holds me tight. Moises doesn't dance. He leans against a wall and bounces his head to the beat while he stares at me. I close my eyes but Moises's face appears in my thoughts and I'm filled with guilt.

The music switches from rap to reggae. The room is stuffed with bodies gyrating as one. Nick grinds in but I pull away.

"I need some air," I say. I can't keep this up, not with Moises steps away.

"Let's go for a walk." Nick grabs a blanket from an outdoor chest and produces a bottle of vodka and two plastic cups. We walk past Moises, who's now standing by the door. I keep my eyes to the ground.

"Margot," Moises says.

"Something up?" Nick asks.

"Naw, nothing is up," Moises says. "I'm heading back into the city. Margot, there's room for you in the car. Let me drive you back."

I can't look at him.

"No, I'm staying," I mumble. There's a long pause.

"Good luck then," he says, and walks away.

Nick and I are both shivering. He places his arm around me.

"Here's to the end of summer," he says as he pours me another drink.

"Uh-huh." I take a large gulp.

I've wanted this. Why can't I sink into it and allow the moment to engulf me? When I turn to Nick, I'm relieved to find that the darkness conceals his face. It's easy to be daring in the dark. No accusing eyes. I lean over to him and make the first move. I plan to see this to the end.

His tongue rolls around in my mouth. Clumsy and sloppy. I'm angry about not wanting him more. So I kiss him harder but I still feel nothing. No matter what I do I can't get Moises out of my head.

I pull away and stand. My hand brushes the sand off my legs. What am I doing?

"Are you okay?" he asks.

Nick's smart. Nice. The beach house is insane. I can just imagine what his real home must be like. There are no confusing signals from him. He's everything Moises is not. This is an easy decision. I can do this. I'm not a child.

"Why are you here with me?" I ask.

He probably thinks this is the alcohol talking, and he might be right.

"I like you. I've seen you around," he says. "Serena and Camille said you were cool. Been meaning to talk."

Nick needed the right circumstances to chat me up. The whole package had to be complete. And now it is. I'm perfect. But we're not really talking, are we? That's not the point. I sit down and we kiss again.

This time, he pulls back.

"Let's slow down," he says. "We don't have to rush anything."

But we do. Things gnaw inside me. This is what I can do to keep the truth at bay. I'll do whatever I can to squash my feelings for Moises and my feelings about my actions.

"I want to," I say.

Things move fast. Soon Nick is taking the lead but he doesn't cup my face. His fingers are rough but I keep going. I don't stop. I'm really going to do this. He fumbles with a condom. Everything happens so quickly because I'm willing it. Nick goes along. It hurts, from his kisses on my neck to his body thrusting against me, but it's over quickly. I stand and take the bottle of vodka with me. I need this moment to become one massive blur, to be obliterated from my mind. I leave Nick there as he pulls up his pants.

"Where are you going?" he asks. "Did I do something wrong?"

I don't answer and he doesn't follow. Moises would have made sure I was safe. He would have walked me. Wait, what am I thinking? Moises would never have been invited to this party.

Each step is weighed down by the sand. Or is it the bottle I'm clinging to? I toss the empty bottle and walk back to the crowded party. There's no sign of Freddie or Willie. No sign of Moises.

"Shake that ass!" Serena pulls me to the dance floor. She spins me around and around till I can barely breathe. I'm going to be sick.

"I can't anymore," I plead with her. "I'm so drunk."

"So am I!" Serena screams and laughs like a lunatic. I force laughter until tears stream down my cheeks. Are people staring? No, I'm laughing. That's what they see.

"I need to leave. I think I'm going to throw up."

"Are you crazy!" Serena says. "The music is pumping. You can't go!"

I stumble away from her. I have to find Camille. I need to go before I see Nick and before I throw up and truly make a fool of myself. The line to the bathroom is not that long but I still manage to convince the girl at the front of it to let me cut. Inside the bathroom I splash cold water on my face. I've got to pull myself together. Camille won't help me if I'm sick. I need her to point me in the direction of her house. She told me she lived only a couple of houses away from Nick.

Although it's difficult, I manage to walk up the stairs.

LILLIAM RIVERA

Camille is sitting on a lounge chair with a guy. He's trying to kiss her neck but Camille swats him away every time. I inhale deeply and march up to her.

"Camille, can I talk to you for a second?" I hope she's as drunk as I am. "Do you mind if I head over to your place?"

"Where's Nick? And Serena said some guys you know from the Bronx showed up. What is going on?"

The guy nuzzles her some more. Camille acts like she's annoyed but she loves the attention.

"I left Nick on the beach," I blurt out. I keep my stupid grin on even when I know it's more of a grimace.

"Oh my god! You are a bad bitch," Camille says. "I want to know what happened."

The guy pinches her side and Camille shrieks. He won't stop and I know I have a way out.

"What's the address again?" I say.

"It's Thirteen Twenty-Two Meadow Lane. The green house. Here's the extra key and don't get sick!"

From the balcony, I see Nick talking to Serena. He's searching for me. I've got to go. I sneak out the door.

I'm drunk and on some destructive path. The houses along the beach look exactly the same but I eventually find Camille's house. On the walk I throw up twice. I open the door and don't bother looking for a light switch. I find the couch and fling myself onto it. The room turns and turns. Sand has invaded every crevice of my body. I try not to be sick again.

On paper, my first time could very well be described as romantic. I was with a sweet boy on the beach, I could say, with the waves crashing and a half-moon. The reality is more like a wrestling match played on fast forward with me trying to avoid Nick's sloppy tongue. I thought being with Nick would banish thoughts of Moises. That didn't happen. What I have to show for my first time is sand up my ass and emptiness.

CHAPTER 19

There is not enough water to wash down the taste of bile in my mouth. I couldn't escape the Hamptons quickly enough. I snuck out before anyone woke up, ordered a cab to take me to the station, and left. I want to forget what happened last night and hide in my room.

Sometime during the night, I overheard Camille and Serena talking about my hookup with Nick. While I pretended to sleep, they argued over which one deserved credit. Serena believes Nick and I make a great couple. Camille insists that he's nothing but the jump-off and that I will now be open to other Somerset possibilities. The topic soon switched over to the sluttiest girl at the party.

Funny how at any other time I would have been happy to hear Serena and Camille talk about me. This should be my moment. I got the social props I've been working toward. Instead, I'm disgusted with myself.

I approach my house and hear voices yelling out in anger. There's a temptation to turn right back to the train station but I accept this as another form of punishment for my mistakes. I go in.

"Pero Victor!" Mami is in the family room with her hands pressed against her hips. My father's back is to her.

"He's been with you for twenty years. You know he has other mouths to feed." Mami grabs his arm. Her voice gets louder. "How is he supposed to take care of his family? Did you ever think about that?"

"Ya. Stick to what you know: the house, the kids." He pushes past her and straight into his office. He slams the door shut.

Mami's erect posture drops into a slouch. She presses her hand against her forehead and brushes her hair back. This has been going on for some time. I walked in at the tail end. She's unaware of my presence.

"Mami," I say gently so as not to startle her. "What's going on?"

She looks at me as if she doesn't recognize me. Then she grabs a towel from behind the bar and wipes it down.

"What happened?"

"Your father is making a big mistake." She mumbles to herself some more as if I'm not in the room. "He used to rely on me for every decision regarding that place. Y ahora qué? Nothing. I just don't know. Life was easier when we had one small supermarket. Simple."

"Mami, you're not telling me anything," I say. "What's going on?"

She looks up for a second but returns to polishing the corner of the bar.

"Mami?"

"I'm busy. Please bring down your laundry."

It's useless. She's lost in memories of the past. I've seen the pictures of the three of them—Mami, Papi, and Junior posed in front of the supermarket. Life may have been easier back then but she fails to remember that I wasn't around. Mami wants to go back in time. Does she even care how that makes me feel?

I wait a few minutes before heading over to Papi's office. Unlike Mami, he'll talk. Before entering, I announce myself. I don't want him to think Mami is back to rage some more.

"La Princesa," he says with his arms open. A wave of emotion washes over me. I didn't realize how much I needed a hug.

"We both have very sad faces." He lifts my chin up. "I can afford to be sad but you, you're too young."

Papi leans his head on mine, something he used to do when I was little. He would lean on it until I couldn't bear the weight. There's a pit in my stomach. Bad things always come in threes. First Moises. Then my moment at the beach with Nick. What else can make this weekend worse?

"You should know this before heading back to work on Monday," Papi says. "I had to let Oscar go."

This can't be right. Oscar's been with Papi since he started Sanchez & Sons. They knew each other from back on the island. Oscar technically runs the place. There must be a mistake.

"Why?" I ask.

"He's been stealing money for some time and when I confronted him he denied it," Papi says. "Plus, there were some stock discrepancies that didn't add up."

Stock discrepancies. Missing beer cases. This is my fault. I got Oscar fired. He could have easily explained to Papi that I was the one who stole the cases of beer but he didn't. Oscar protected me.

"That can't be right. Why would he steal?" I say. "He loves us."

"Junior brought it to my attention. It makes sense," Papi says. "Now tell me what you did this weekend so that you can cheer me up."

"But what's going to happen to him? What about his family?"

"We discovered who the thief is and we handled it. It's fine. Things happen."

The shame I feel is so deep that it fills the room.

"But Papi, maybe I made a mistake. I probably made an error when I was checking the stock. Jasmine didn't train me. I'm positive it's my fault."

"There's no excuse for what he did," Papi says. "If there's no trust, there's nothing. The only people I can trust are family. You understand that now, don't you? I only have you two kids to mind the store."

His Princesa can do no wrong. Maybe she can steal his credit card and charge up clothes but worse than that? He doesn't know me. I could come clean right now. I could tell Papi I was the one who stole the beers and that Oscar is completely innocent. But I don't say a word. I'm too much of a coward. This mask I wear that conceals my true self, I will keep it on forever at the cost of Oscar, Moises, and everyone.

"Hey, hey. What's going on here?" Papi holds me tight. "There's no need for tears. Oscar will find another job. Everything will work out."

No, it won't.

Junior's bedroom door is ajar. A towel hangs loosely around his waist and I can see his bones. I can actually count his ribs. This is the thinnest I've ever seen him.

"Jesus, you are so skinny." I touch his scrawny arm.

"It's hard to eat when you got people stealing your food." He quickly pulls on a long-sleeved shirt. "Those tears better not be for Oscar."

Junior doesn't look right. His clothes are so baggy on him. "Are you sick?"

"That son of a bitch has been wiping us clean for months. You think I could eat knowing that?" Junior talks at a rapid speed. His face is flushed but I can't tell if that's from the shower or from something else.

"I had my suspicions about Oscar but Papi wasn't going to be believe me until I had proof. If that fucker was struggling, he should have spoken up. He didn't just fuck our father. Oscar fucked our whole family." Junior's once-muscular arms thrash around like long toothpicks. "He fucked you over."

My stomach churns. His words make me dizzy. Junior is on something and I can't figure out what. Or maybe it's the combination of my hangover and the news of Oscar that makes me feel sick again. It's too much.

"How did you find out?" I ask.

"It doesn't matter how I found out. I should have known right away. He never wanted me to work there. Oscar was always pissing on my ideas. See, that's what he gets."

"What is going on with you? You're scaring me," I say. "Maybe you should go see a doctor. About your weight?"

"What the fuck are you talking about?" He checks his phone and taps on it with anger. "Did you come in here to accuse me of something? You're just like Papi. Always thinking the worst of me."

LILLIAM RIVERA

"It's not true. I'm worried."

"You don't give a shit about anyone." Junior is right in my face. "Go back to your little sheltered world, Princesa."

Where does this anger come from? It's like that time he almost ripped my arm off when he accused me of talking to Moises. I slam the door behind me. My only safe haven is my bedroom.

Everyone in this house hides behind closed doors. We build fortresses to bar people from scaling the walls and getting in. But even with the amount of time we spend sheltering ourselves there's no way of concealing our problems.

Life took a horrible turn somewhere. Oscar is fired. Junior is wasting away, and me . . . I don't know a thing about people and the actions they take. Why did Oscar protect me? I don't believe for a second that he stole money. He could have easily told on me. And then there's Moises. Why did he say the things he said to me on the beach? I will never understand.

218

CHAPTER 20

Before the store opens, Papi gathers the workers and makes the official announcement. A longtime produce clerk demands to see the evidence that got Oscar fired. The butcher calms him down and advises him that arguing with the boss may not be the smartest thing to do, not when everyone's job is on the line. Because if Oscar is not safe, no one is.

A cashierista starts to cry.

"Shut up with that crying!" Jasmine yells. The hate flows freely.

"Junior will take on Oscar's responsibilities," Papi says, eager to dismiss the mob that forms right in front of him.

"How's that gonna work if he's never here and when he is, he's busy with the girls?" A young stock boy dares to speak his mind.

Papi and Junior glare back at him, an act that should instill fear, but the stock boy doesn't back down. He's voicing what's on everyone's mind.

"If you don't like it, you can pick up your last check," Junior threatens. Spoken like a true dictator. I have to give him points for at least dressing the part in a suit. He promised Papi he would bring his A game from now on. If by A game he means rule by intimidation, he's well on his way.

"Now if there aren't any other questions, I'll be in the office," Papi says. He turns his back on them.

Some of the workers give me the evil eye. They speak loudly, for my benefit, about how Oscar is the breadwinner. His wife stays at home to tend to the kids.

"How is he supposed to survive?" they ask, clucking their tongues.

"It must be nice," a cashierista says to me.

"Excuse me?"

"Pues nada. Just that it must be nice. Gozando de la vida, without worrying about how to pay the bills. Your life is without complaints. Sin problemas."

I sink my head and utter the only thing I'm capable of saying: "Sorry."

She doesn't hear me. The cashierista is too busy attacking my family. I take cover in the back aisle, where I stock and restock a shelf. From my safe perch, I witness extreme emotions vibrating throughout the store, some employees wanting to appease Papi to keep their jobs and others sabotaging Junior's appointed role as "Oscar Dos." Even the always-verbal Dominic quietly stocks the shelves next to me. Not a crude joke or a lewd rap song from him.

My phone explodes with texts from Serena and Camille on how Nick looks sad and lonely. They consider my Hamptons disappearance a good tactic. Leave him wanting more is what Camille said yesterday.

It's easy to sound excited via text. A few exclamation points can cover my true feelings. Serena and Camille know about Nick's call to me last night. I didn't answer the phone. They advised me not to respond right away. To wait a couple of days. Let Nick sweat, Serena said. I follow their suggestions like a mindless robot.

"Doña Sanchez! Hace tiempo que no te veo por aquí!" Rosa exclaims.

Mami holds several trays of food. She wears a floral sheath dress with high heels. Her hair and makeup are immaculate. I don't know why she's here but she bears gifts and an unnatural smile.

Papi rushes downstairs but Mami ignores him. It's clear from her cold reception that this visit was not planned. Papi is as shocked as I am. The last time Mami came to the supermarket was during Easter. She only visits during major holidays. This is some fluke.

"Tu. Nena. Take these and set them up in the break

room." Mami dumps the trays on Jasmine without even so much as a greeting. So cold.

Jasmine scowls at Papi as if he should control Mami. He does nothing. I wait for Jasmine to respond with her usual repertoire of curses but she doesn't. Instead, she snaps her gum and strolls to the back. It's so weird. Why would she take that from her? Jasmine has never been one to keep quiet. Oscar's news, and now Mami's visit, is throwing everyone off their game, including Jasmine.

Although Mami rarely makes appearances at the store, she's well aware of everyone's history—whether their child started high school, if another is expecting a baby. Mami shares small anecdotes with each person that prove she remembers them intimately. Although I work with these people, I don't know half of what she knows about them.

"Muchacha, tú estás comiendo?" The cashieristas measure her thin arms. Mami shoos them away, insisting that she's fine.

"Claro que sí," she says. They tease her but there's nothing mean behind it. The early wave of hostility slowly melts away. She's the much-needed distraction. Add the fact that Mami brought food and people are like, "Oscar who?"

"Margot, can you make sure that girl back there knows what she's doing?" She pats my shoulder.

"Jesus, Mom," I say. "Her name is Jasmine."

She pushes me along.

The break room is converted into a mini-buffet with burners lit up to keep the delicious food heated. There's a tray of arroz con gandules. Another tray of roasted pork with garlic. Fried sweet plantains. Alcapurrias and empanadas. Mami did not skimp. I find Jasmine searching for paper plates.

"What the hell is she doing here?"

"Mami wants to treat everyone to lunch," I say, but I wonder the same thing. Mami hates the drive here but the whole thing with Oscar must have gotten to her. The arguments with Papi lasted throughout the night until eventually he drove off. "Why are you acting nervous?"

"I'm not nervous!" Jasmine says. "I just don't like surprises."

"Neither do I."

I help Jasmine fold napkins. We locate a small bouquet of fake flowers and place it near the food. Not sure why I bother. The minute Mami inspects this, she'll find something wrong. Jasmine's nervousness is contagious.

"I need to work. I'm not the maid." Jasmine uses a napkin to soak up a bit of sauce that's spilled out from one of the trays. She's gained a bit of weight. Most people wouldn't be able to tell that she's pregnant but the signs are obvious to me. Her hips are more pronounced. And if it's possible, her mood swings are even more intense.

Just as Jasmine approves the display, Mami sweeps into the room.

"We need some coffee and pastries. Here." She rummages through her purse. Mami employs the same tone she uses with our housekeeper, Yolanda, not asking but ordering Jasmine to do her bidding. "Go next door and bring two dozen of their desserts. We need something freshly baked, not the dull pastries we sell here. You do know how many are in a dozen?"

Mami then turns to me and says, "Your father should employ people with at least a high school education."

Jasmine's face turns bright red. So does mine. But Jasmine does nothing to defend herself. I'm both embarrassed and confused by Mami's cruelty and Jasmine's sudden cowardice. What is going on?

"Bueno, nena. I don't have all day." Mami dangles the money in front of her face.

Jasmine snatches it and stomps out of the room.

"What's your problem?" I yell. "Why are you being so mean to her? What has Jasmine ever done to you?"

Mami takes the fake flowers and places them back on the shelf where I found them. She folds the napkins into fans and finds a pitcher of water. She's undone our efforts in one fell swoop.

"Esa idiota barely finished elementary school. We're lucky she can count to ten." Mami's pleased with her decorative napkins. "Now hand me those cups."

I throw the cups on the table, intentionally ruining her silly display.

"Jasmine is right, you're so full of yourself."

Before I can walk away, Mami takes hold of my arm.

"Fix this right now."

"No! Fix it yourself."

"Don't ever take the side of strangers over family. Ever. Come over here and fix this now." She pinches my arm. This visit has nothing to do with Oscar. She must know about Jasmine being pregnant. Maybe Junior came clean. This is her way of lashing out about it without confronting the two people outright. My family is so corrupt.

"The person you should be hurting is not here. Go attack Junior. He's the one to blame."

Mami lets go. Her hands tremble.

"El que hace lo paga." She goes back to the table.

"What does that even mean? The person who does it pays for it? You're talking in riddles!"

I turn quiet when Jasmine returns with the baked goods. She places the box and the money on the table.

"You can keep the change," Mami says.

"No gracias, Señora Sanchez. Your husband pays me enough." They stare at each other as if they're cocking their guns, ready to shoot. Jasmine blinks and leaves.

Mami grabs a plate.

"Quieres pernil?" She acts as if the whole exchange with Jasmine never happened. Mami blames her without once considering Junior is at fault too. It's so typical to condemn the girl. Jasmine is the bad person, the one who "seduced" Junior, while my brother is absolved of any wrongdoing. He gets away with it.

"I'm not hungry." I leave her with her banquet of total BS.

Unlike the rest of the workers, who enjoy the feast, Jasmine refuses to take any breaks. She even works through her lunch hour.

Papi stays in seclusion too. He never leaves his office, which is for the best since Mami's charm works on the others. The workers feel safe enough to state how upset they are and she offers a shoulder. Junior, on the other hand, tries to force everyone back to work. No one follows his orders, not while Mami is there to make things right with food and soothing conversations. She stays at the store for another hour and urges everyone to take home leftovers.

Mami doesn't fool me with her generous display, not after what she did to Jasmine. This performance is for the others, to show that we're a united family that will take care of them. We will, but only to a certain degree.

Somewhere out there Moises shakes his head.

CHAPTER 23

Rain pelts the kitchen window. The wind picks up speed and thrashes against the trees in the backyard. It's a sure indication that summer is near its end. The crummy weather is a perfect excuse to stay home and avoid everyone. But some people are unavoidable.

"Wassup, sistah?" Junior grabs a French fry off my plate.

"Why aren't you closing the store?" I ask.

"I got business to attend to. Besides, everyone is on point at that place," he says. "I'm meeting Ray to check out this new club by Fordham University. Rich college students means money to spend."

Throughout the week, my brother has transformed into the perfect Sanchez manager. He comes to work early. He's even started to employ a clipboard, jotting down ideas or customer complaints, a plan I suggested to Papi a long time ago. But I know what's up. It's an act, a way for him to butter up Papi to invest in that bar. Who knows? Maybe Papi will change his mind now that Junior is doing the right thing for once.

"What are you doing home, looking mopey?" Junior asks. "Don't you have any plans?"

I push away my plate. It's Saturday night and everyone has somewhere to go, including Mami, who was picked up early by a friend to attend some sort of Bible study. We've never been religious but as of late, Mami's been going to church, perhaps as an act of penance for her recent malicious ways. She should, anyway.

Junior shoves a couple more fries in his mouth.

"You've been with that face for days," he says.

"How can you be so happy with what's going on with Jasmine and Oscar? You are so oblivious."

"That's not true. I'm trying to do right by people. Listen, Jasmine refuses to talk to me every time I approach her. I can't force her to tell me what's wrong," he says. "I know we haven't been nice to each other in a long time but I'm still your big brother."

I laugh bitterly. "Are you kidding me? You've been a complete jerk to me this summer. I don't even know why I'm talking to you right now. So what if you're in a good mood? Your happiness is not contagious."

Guilt invades his face. "You're right. I haven't been nice but I've been getting it from both sides. You know how it's been. Things are settling down now. Papi will see I can handle the supermarket and he'll forget about Oscar. He'll come around with the bar. Just wait."

Junior lists his plans for world domination without the slightest clue that I'm no longer listening. After a while, he stops. If there's no audience, there's no point in trying to impress. I throw out the rest of my dinner and leave. Let Junior live in his own delusional bubble.

The only thing left to do is wait for school to start. Only two weeks remain in my ten-week supermarket sentence. Soon I'll be back at Somerset but even that prospect doesn't hold much hope. The thought of having to perform my fake act depresses me. So much of my time and energy has been invested in becoming this wannabe, but I'm no longer interested in that person or the final outcome. I want my life to rewind to two years ago when I cared less about impressing other people and more about having fun.

On my dresser is a picture of Elizabeth when we went to Playland one summer. We're dressed in old-fashioned get-ups. She's Calamity Jane and I'm Buffalo Bill. The costumes were way too big for our small frames. We were both around twelve. Why does that seem so long ago? I haven't spoken to her since the concert. She's probably already heard what went down with Moises and Freddie. No doubt Moises

made a move on her after the way I flat-out rejected him. I
fool myself into thinking that these hypothetical scenarios
don't bother me and that my moving on from Elizabeth is a
sign of maturity. But I miss her.

There's a soft rap at my bedroom door. Junior pokes his
head in.

"Here."

A glint of gold lands on my pillow. I pick it up.

A solid gold Tiffany heart with the word PRINCESA
engraved on the back hangs from a delicate necklace strand.
It's stunning. Every year for my birthday, my parents buy
me jewelry from Tiffany. But my birthday is not for another
two months. Am I being punked in some way? Junior comes
over by me to admire it.

"What's this for?"

"I planned to give it to you on your birthday but what
the hell," he says.

I caress the heart. There's no way he could afford a Tiffany on his own. It's not possible.

"But why? How?"

"Now you can't wish me dead or that necklace will
burn your skin off." He chuckles. "I'm telling you, things
are going to be different. I'm going to be a better person, a
better brother to you. Now stop moping around and cheer
the hell up."

I can't help but love it. This is something to brag about

come September. But there it is again: my desire to be liked, not for me, but for what I can acquire. Some superficial label. I will never stop trying.

"This is crazy. I can't take this. It's a Tiffany! There's no way you can afford this."

"It's nicer than what those jerks get you, right? See, your brother knows how to take care of you." He still tries to one-up my parents. Even this selfless act comes in the form of a competition.

"This is too much," I say.

"Yeah, yeah, yeah. Shut up and take it."

"But Junior . . ."

He steals a pack of gum on his way out with a grin that only dumb girls could love.

This charm blows the necklace Mami gave me last year out of the water. Still, it doesn't make sense. It's one thing to feel guilty but it's quite another to buy a Tiffany for your sister. Even I would never do that if I had the money. How much could this have cost him? I go online to see for myself.

Jesus. The heart charm is listed at $600 with a chain at $225. My brother may have expensive taste for himself but not for me. There's no way he would drop that much money on me. Either (a) this necklace isn't a true Tiffany, (b) it is and it's totally stolen, or (c) he's the best brother ever. I aim to find out.

"Hey, Junior!"

There's no answer. I run downstairs to see if I can catch him before he leaves but I'm too late. There must be a receipt somewhere. I head to his room. The door is always locked but Mami keeps a spare key in a jar.

Junior's clothes are strewn over the bed and on the floor. He tossed me the necklace without allowing me the opportunity of opening the signature blue Tiffany box. He probably got it off someone selling it on the street. Random guys come to the supermarket and try to sell bootleg DVDs of movies currently out in theaters or "expensive" watches. Depending on his mood, Papi will either chase them out of the store or buy a couple of movies. This necklace has to be a fake.

On top of Junior's dresser rest the pack of gum he stole, an empty box of cigarettes, and several matchbooks. I search the wastebasket. Nothing. I focus on the bottom drawers and work my way up. Then I make my way underneath the bed. With my haphazard search method, I'm able to locate a couple of joints and a dime bag hidden in a shoe box. But otherwise no luck. I look for a piece of paper, something that proves the necklace is a Tiffany and not a Riffany or a Kiffany.

The windows are shut and I sneeze from the dust. I finally hit the closet. It's a sea of clothes, coordinated by color. That's one thing we both share, a sense of fashion organization. I push aside a row of slacks and reach a back shelf that holds what look like important files. Receipts from dinners and nightclub admission stubs are bundled together with a rubber band. Still not what I want.

Just as I'm about to give up my toe hits something with a loud thump. It's hidden far back in the closet but after jostling a few items around, I'm able to get a firm grip. I place the long aluminum box on Junior's bed. There's no lock on it. I open it.

The box is filled with money, rolls upon rolls of cash. My heart sinks, then pounds. I've never seen so much money in one place. There are bills in amounts I've never possessed. My hands waver in front of the money as if the bills themselves will turn around and bite me.

"What the fuck." I take the rolls out one by one and arrange them on the bed.

That's where I find the unthinkable. Beneath the cash are tiny plastic baggies full of rocks. Rocks and white powder. There are so many.

Jesus. Oh my god. This is how he could afford a Tiffany. Drugs.

Right in the corner of the box are a well-used pipe and several lighters. The room seems to tilt and then everything slants into place. Junior's sudden weight loss. His extreme actions. His disheveled appearance. It makes sense. He's the thief.

Papi. I've got to tell Papi.

I dial his number but no one answers. It's close to ten. Papi always locks up by eleven on Saturdays. There's no way I can keep this in. He'll know what to do. I scoop up a couple of the baggies, place the money in the box, and put the box back in the closet where I found it. I run downstairs, hop on my bike, and head to the train station.

I can't think straight.

CHAPTER 22

The number of times I call Papi borders on stalker territory. Every time, it goes straight to his voice mail. I can't miss him. I'm trying again when I notice a cop patrolling the platform. He nods hello at me. I'm holding god knows what kind of drugs. My night can't end with a trip to jail.

I pray for this to be a huge mistake. Maybe Junior's holding this stuff for someone else or he's been forced to against his will. But who am I kidding? Junior's been out of control for some time. What goes through his head? Drugs. There are so many ways to make money. He must have watched *Scarface* one too many times. I've seen the end of that movie. Not pretty.

When the train finally arrives, it goes at a deadly slow pace, stopping at every station. I'm left with my thoughts, running through the signs that pointed to Junior's problems. It plays out like a corny antidrug PSA. We ignored them. The fact that he lost weight and his insane mood swings. Junior even pulled out that big wad of cash on me like he was Pitbull's manager. What a joke! I had my suspicions but I denied them.

And Oscar? We both screwed him. From the minute I stepped into the supermarket Oscar made me feel welcome. He was always fair. If Oscar scolded you, you deserved it. But he became our sucker. We both lied through our straight white teeth and let him take the fall for us.

I try Papi again but there's no cell phone service.

I finally reach the Yankee Stadium station. Only a few more blocks. The rain has stopped and what remains is an imposing heat. The air feels heavy. Dirty. Nothing can combat the intense swelter. I should try to take a bus but there is a small crowd waiting. It's going to be a while. I decide to walk instead. Smells of gasoline and melting tar hit me as I wait at a red light.

"Where you going, mama?" a man yells from the sidewalk. "I'll go with you."

Eager to get away from the pervert, I cross the street and a gypsy cab almost hits me. I've got to calm down. Papi will know what to do. Junior is in desperate need of saving. The good news is Oscar can come back. The supermarket can return to normal. No more drama. I'll soon be back at school and the horrible Sanchez kids with their evil selfish ways will no longer create havoc in the South Bronx. Papi should never have forced us to work there. It's obvious we can't handle it.

I finally reach the front of the supermarket. The light from the corner streetlamp reflects off the SANCHEZ & SONS sign. It's ten past eleven. There's still a chance that I can catch Papi.

A group of guys lean against the wall. It's so strange to see them out here at night and to see the supermarket so desolate. Everything seems so out of place. My eyes still search for Moises, a stupid habit that does nothing to comfort me. He can't help. No one can. This is a family affair and for once I totally understand what Papi and Mami constantly drill into us: There is only the family and no one else.

A boy from the group recognizes me. "It's closed," he says.

"Did you see my father leave?" I ask. "Mr. Sanchez?"

The guy shakes his head. Even with the doors locked, I pound away in the hope that Papi's still in the office. I press my face to the window. There's no answer. I start the long walk around the block to the back of the store. He might be still parked, about to drive home. Why doesn't he answer his damn phone? I don't understand people who have a cell phone and refuse to check it every five minutes like a normal person. This trip can't be a complete waste of time. I pick up the pace.

Relief comes over me as I notice Papi's car at the far end of the lot. Thank god. I can just about make out his head in the car. He's probably listening to the roughly twenty phone messages I left him and wondering what the hell is wrong.

"Papi!"

I wave to him but he doesn't move. I walk even faster. His car windows are closed. It's too hot for that. He must be suffocating. Has he fallen asleep? Maybe he's sick. I run to the car, ready to smash the window open. But as I get nearer I see that he's not alone. There's someone else in the car.

And his hand . . . His hand is caressing the person's cheek.

My feet turn to cement. I fight to register what's going on, for my brain to make the connection with what my eyes see. I can't look away. I know exactly what's happening. He is kissing this person and I can't move although everything inside me screams to. My cell phone slips from my hand and crashes to the ground. The sound startles Jasmine.

Oh my god. It's Jasmine. She's in the car.

My feet turn to take me as far away as possible from that, from them. My name is called. Footsteps. Papi catches up to me.

"What are you doing here?" he asks. He struggles to tuck his shirt back into his pants. "Margot, answer me."

I'm going to be sick. A car door slams shut. Jasmine is either out of the car or has closed the door to stay in. I want to get out of here. I don't want to answer his questions and watch him adjusts his pants. Where do I look? Not at him. Not at the floor. He grips my arm and jerks me. I yank back. The anger finally reaches the surface and joins the present moment.

"How could you do this?" I scream. "To Mami? To us?"

"There's no reason for you to be here at this hour," he says. "Why aren't you home?"

"Stop asking me questions!" I'm furious.

"Calm down. This is a private matter. You need to go home. It's late."

"Private? You're in a parking lot!" I'm so loud that the boys from out front stroll back to check the commotion. "She works for you. Do you pay her extra for this? Is this what overtime means? At least pay for a hotel."

"Keep your voice down. Let's go inside and talk about this." Papi's unable to look me in the eye. Instead, he walks toward me as if diminishing the distance between us will keep the outrage from spilling out. But I can't be contained.

"You're married. Does that mean anything to you? You're disgusting. A cerdo. A pig." The insults tumble out as quickly as the tears.

"Hey, are you all right?" the boy from earlier asks. His buddies surround us now. An audience to witness Papi's vulgar ways.

"Everything is fine. Just an argument," Papi says like a

true showman. He can't afford any public embarrassments. I completely lose it and curse at him, something I've never done before.

"Enough, Princesa," he says. "I want you inside the supermarket right now." He's mad but he has no right. I won't let him hide behind his stupid reputation. I'm peeling off his bullshit of a mask, of being the loving father and husband. With each step Papi takes I let out another string of insults.

"You liar. You piece of shit. You are nothing but a sucio."

He tries his best to shush me. The neighborhood guys don't turn away even when Papi tells them this is a personal matter. Why should they? This is better than TV, better than watching the cars drive by.

"What's it like, Papi? Huh?" I say. "What's it like to have your employee fuck you in your car?"

Papi lunges at me. I try to avoid him but I trip and fall to the ground.

A collective hush falls over everyone until a guy from the group says, "Damn, that's fucked up."

"Margot, let's go inside," Papi pleads, desperate to conceal this scene from the people he serves. He offers me a hand to help me back up on my feet.

"Don't touch me." I pick myself up and storm away. Papi runs after me. He looks insane as he pulls my arm. I wrestle to try to break free.

"Leave her alone!" someone yells. And with that, Papi comes to his senses and lets go of me. He can't be seen this way. Unraveled. He has a rep to uphold. I barrel out of there. I don't know where I'm going but I need to get away.

Images flash in my head. Jasmine. Papi. I can't even begin to process it. A car alarm goes off and I jump from the noise. My heart is about to come out of my body. I'm so upset but I just keep walking. I don't know where I am. Nothing looks familiar. I finally stop in front of a community garden. The heat is so oppressive that it's hard for me to breathe. I find a bench and sit.

Unlike my father, I have no qualms about showing random people who walk by how I feel. They stare as if whatever ails me might also contaminate them. I try to calm down but it's impossible. I reach inside my purse and realize that my phone is still on the ground in the supermarket parking lot. But who would I even call? Serena and Camille wouldn't understand. It's too embarrassing.

I sit there crying, reimagining my life into a more favorable conclusion. In my ideal, my brother stays in college and graduates. Oscar still works for us and I spend my summer far away from here. But no matter how hard I try to reconfigure the events, Jasmine still ends up in the front seat of Papi's car.

What a hypocrite. Papi hides behind long-winded speeches showing how perfect he is. He looked down on

Moises while fucking Jasmine. What a fool I was to listen to her sob story the other day. I'm the clueless girl who couldn't figure out that her brother is a thief and an addict while her father is the true player of the family.

Wait.

I'm a liar too. I used Nick that night. Maybe I did him a favor with the beers but the rest of it? That was me. Truth be told, I used Moises too. I tried to play him the night we hung out on the roof. I knew deep down my friends and family would never accept him. And when I got to know him, I wasn't brave enough to allow myself to get closer. Instead, I turned to Nick. How different am I than my father, than my brother? I'm well on my way to following in their footsteps.

I don't want this family history. I have to believe I have a choice. But what if it's in my blood? Can I keep from making the same mistakes? I'm not sure.

There's no way of telling what time it is. It must be late. I search for the nearest train station. I don't know what I'm doing.

CHAPTER 23

The streets are desolate. Barely anyone around. I need to unburden myself, to share what happened with someone else, because right now it feels like a bad dream. I lean my bike in front of Elizabeth's house but fear keeps me from entering. Why am I hesitating? Humiliation. My family is a joke and a part of me wants to deny what happened. It would be easier to pretend everything is fine. Simpler to head back home, but only more heartache awaits me there.

Elizabeth is dabbing a bit of paint onto a canvas in her studio. She takes a few steps back to look at her work and then continues. The Boogaloo Bad Boys are playing on her radio. I knew she'd be up. She always likes to paint at night. I'm sort of gambling here. She can turn me away. I deserve the brush-off but I pray she doesn't give it to me because I need her.

I gather what little courage I can and knock on the door.

"Ma, I'm working." Elizabeth doesn't turn away from her canvas. I've always been jealous of how much time she dedicates to her art. "I'm an artist," she'd say with such conviction. I've never been sure of anything.

"Elizabeth," I mumble. My throat is raw. I'm raw right down to my fingertips. Elizabeth doesn't conceal her shock.

"What happened?" she asks. "Are you okay?"

Everything wells up again. Where to begin? It's too painful. I'm taken right back to the supermarket. To him. To Jasmine's face.

"I'm not hurt. Can I please sit here?" I say. "I won't bother you."

Elizabeth turns the music down.

"Sure," she says, and places a bottle of water on the table next to the futon sofa. There's a box of tissues and I proceed to empty it. After a few minutes, Elizabeth returns to her canvas and paints. The canvas displays the outline of kids splashing around in front of a hydrant. Their wide grins posed in screams of delight. I recognize the area. It's Poe Park, the park she took me to the day we ran into Moises. It was the last time she and I spoke.

We stay like this for a long time.

"Sometimes it's better to say whatever is on your mind really quick," Elizabeth eventually says. "Mom swears it's bad for your body to keep it in. Like a cancer. You have to get it out as soon as possible."

I take a couple of deep breaths.

Elizabeth is the only person I can trust right now. Not Serena and Camille. Papi's disgusting act and Junior's addiction are a reflection of the type of family I come from. I could never admit any of this to them. Elizabeth won't judge. I gulp down some water and begin.

"I caught Papi kissing some girl from work." Elizabeth puts down her paintbrush and motions for me to give her the bottle.

"Wow," she says, then takes a sip.

"Yeah." I can't even make a joke about it. How he offers a full benefits package for the workers there. How the "S" in "Sanchez" stands for "suck." The jokes are there but I'm too numb to offer any punch lines.

"Does your mom know?"

"I think she knows something. The way she treated Jasmine the other day. Like dirt. Worse than dirt," I say. "Jasmine. That's her name."

Who knows how long this thing has been going on, but there's no doubt that Mami knew about it. That trip to the supermarket had everything to do with Papi. The way she tossed that money to Jasmine like she was a whore and those late-night talks to her sisters in Puerto Rico. The arguments and the sadness. I'm probably the only person in the family who hasn't figured out that their marriage is falling apart. Somewhere inside I knew things were bad but I thought they weren't getting along because of the missing money and the problems with Junior. I didn't think past that.

"When I caught him, Papi got angry with me. Can you believe it?"

Elizabeth shakes her head but she doesn't offer anything more than that. No exclamations. She listens but her expression is bland or maybe guarded. I want her to be as floored as I am. I keep giving her more details. Maybe it's the way I present the story.

"Jasmine has been working at the supermarket for years. She's older than us but not by much. Papi always warned me not to get too close to the people there, that we're better than them, and look at what he does. In the parking lot of all places."

The longer Elizabeth stays quiet, the more worked up I get. When will she freak out about it like I'm freaking out right now? Anything but this blank expression.

"I've been walking around with blinders on," I say. "Not really seeing what's going on right in front of me. I've been clueless."

Still nothing. I can't take it. Why is Elizabeth acting so cold? The sadness I felt before I came into her studio transforms into anger. If Elizabeth doesn't say something soon I'll go crazy.

"Did you hear what I said?"

"I'm listening," she says.

"Then why are you acting as if I'm reading a history book to you?" I'm so upset. I want her to be my friend. Why can't she do that? "Maybe you knew Papi was banging Jasmine. Is that it? This isn't news to you? If you know something, tell me. A friend is supposed to share everything. No matter what."

"A friend." Elizabeth repeats the word. "You come over here after I don't know how many days of not speaking to me. And now you accuse me of not being a good friend. But friendship isn't about that."

I can't believe Elizabeth's turning my drama around to attack me. It's true that I haven't been around but it's not my fault.

"You've been acting like such a user," she says.

"I'm not a user."

"What do you call that whole thing that went down with Freddie and the cases of beer?" she says.

"What did he say?" I can't believe Freddie told her my business. That party will forever haunt me. "It was nothing. I didn't make him do anything. It was a stupid mistake."

"You never even bothered to ask if I wanted to go to that party but you invited Freddie, who you just met the other day. I'm so tired of trying."

She says this with a calm voice.

"You don't understand the pressure I've been under. It's been hard to keep up the . . ." I stop talking. I sound like

Junior. Excuses are meaningless. I don't know how to be a friend without the act somehow benefiting me.

"You're not the only person in this world," Elizabeth says. "Everyone hurts and everyone messes up. I just never thought you would be one of those people who would hurt me. You know, you never once introduced me to your new friends. And that day at the park? You just left."

I don't know what to say. I thought separating my Somerset life and my home life made sense.

"It took a while but I dealt with that," she says. "Now I have friends who aren't ashamed of me."

"I'm not ashamed of you. I thought you hated my friends from Somerset. Why would you want to go to the Hamptons? It was just some stupid party. You would have hated everything about it."

"How would you know? You never gave me a chance." She stops and sighs. "I feel bad that you caught your father doing that. That's horrible. But I don't know . . . Never mind."

Elizabeth thrusts her paintbrush into a cup and cleans up. The canvas, which apparently doesn't weigh much, is placed against a wall. I offered up this horrid story and expected to receive understanding. Instead, Elizabeth has finally voiced her feelings of betrayal. There's nothing I can say to make things right. There aren't enough apologies.

Elizabeth washes her hands at the sink and dries them

with a towel. "Stay as long as you want," she says. "Just don't forget to lock the door behind you when you leave."

I watch her head back to the house. It's true. I have been ashamed of her. I wasn't protecting her from my friends at Somerset. That was a lie. I thought if I aligned myself with people who seemed better than me I could transform myself. That is the truth. There's a cost to those schemes.

There's another thing. That day at the park was the first time Elizabeth seemed cooler than me. She talked to Moises and his friends without any hang-ups. It was easy to brush off that moment as being a fluke. Elizabeth and Moises and his friends are weird. Of course they got along. I told myself that to avoid feeling like an outcast. I can't accept Elizabeth because I can't even accept myself.

The sky turns a light blue. Morning comes. I lay my head down on the futon. It's been a long night and my body feels sore. What will the day bring? More drama. I'm certain of that. But can I change the way I deal with it?

I have to show Elizabeth I can do better. Without the fake front I've always used, what will be left of me? Am I worth more than that? I want to believe that it's possible, that my own voice will come out. I can try.

I'll rest here for a couple of hours and then figure out my next step.

CHAPTER 24

Papi's car is not in the driveway or in the garage. Is he afraid to face the family too? I know I am. My mind ran marathons as I tried to rest on Elizabeth's futon. There's no stopping the ongoing list of people I don't want to see, mainly him.

I push my key into the lock and turn the knob.

"Where have you been!" Mami shrieks. She's still in her formal church dress. Anyone else would have at least taken off the heels. She's uncomfortable even in her own home. "Your father's been driving around everywhere looking for you. What is going on?"

The whites of her knuckles grip a cell phone. He hasn't told her. Why would he? There's no point in breaking the news to her. He's not worried about me or concerned about where I am. Papi's scared that I'll alert the world to his nasty business but I don't have to. Mami's silence shows that she's not completely ignorant.

"You know about Jasmine, don't you?" I say.

Mami ignores the question. This is not going to be easy but nothing true ever is.

"Where have you been?" she asks. "Have you been with that boy? We warned you about that. Out on the streets at all hours. It's not the way I . . . the way we raised you."

She takes a couple of steps away from me as I ask the question again.

"Answer me," I say. "Answer me, por favor. Don't shut me out. I want to know. This thing with Jasmine didn't just happen. You knew the day you came to the supermarket."

"You're talking nonsense. Where have you been? Lying to us again. You can't fool me." Mami's fists are clutched to her side. "You are turning into una sucia. A stupid girl with no sense of dignity."

"I wasn't with anyone. Can't say the same about Papi."

She shakes her head as if she can block what I'm saying. I want her to speak to me. I've heard the stories from my aunts when we used to visit Puerto Rico, before the island became too small for Papi. How So-and-so caught her man cheating. The stories never end with "And I left him" or "It destroyed us." There's always some forgiveness bit, an acceptance as if cheating is just part of the family fabric. They used to even joke about it. So-and-so has a chilla on

the side. I didn't even know what a chilla meant until Junior
told me. We laughed because the word sounded funny. Now
the word sounds so abrupt, like a wall. Jasmine, la chilla.

I relent but Mami doesn't want to hear any of it. She
charges past me into the kitchen. She flings open the cabi-
nets and works on the already pristine table. Everything in
this house is immaculate. Everything but our family. There
are not enough cleaning products to take care of our messes.
We are full of flaws.

"Why can't you kids help me keep this place tidy?" she
says. "I say the same thing over and over. No one listens."

"Mami, will you look at me? Please, stop." I take the disinfectant spray bottle from her and place it back in the cabinet.
"I caught Papi with her. With Jasmine. Out in the parking lot."

Mami starts again about the house but this time her
voice cracks. She lets the rag fall from her hand onto the
table.

"Que idiota," she says. Barely a whisper. The lines that
run across her forehead melt away. In their place is a deep
sadness. Her eyes well up and seeing her like that makes my
eyes well up too.

"Why are you still with him?" I ask. "Why don't you
leave?"

"Leave?" she says with anger. "This is my house. I'll never
give this up just because stupid girls put out for your father."

Girls. She said girls.

"There've been others?" Of course. I was foolish to think Jasmine was a one-time deal. Jasmine warned me about the cashieristas. Young and old. Here I thought it was Junior who was making the moves on them. The punches keep coming.

"Margot, men are different. They view sex differently."

"Are you going to tell me that the reason why Papi cheats is because it's part of his genetic makeup?" I can't take it. This can't be coming out of her mouth. There's no way Mami thinks that. She's always warned me not to trust guys. I never knew that included the men in my immediate family. "Don't give me that Latino macho bullshit. You don't believe that."

"Maybe when you're older you'll understand. You're still a child."

She has recited these sentences countless times before but there's no feeling behind them. Trying to shut me up has the opposite effect. I want to scream at the top of my lungs to be heard.

"I'm not a little kid anymore."

She doesn't see me. I reach toward her because it feels as if we're both drowning. I don't want to go under with her. "You know what happens to people who turn away from their problems? They get tripped up. I don't want to fall too. Help me figure this out because right now I need you."

Mami grabs a napkin and methodically cleans up

another invisible stain. She's determined to stand by this cop-out. She lines up the bottles of various spices on the counter like soldiers ready for battle.

"Not everything can be explained away like in one of your lists," she says. "Life isn't that simple."

She turns each of the labels on the spice bottles to face her. Everything in its rightful place. If Mami stopped cleaning she could take a real good look at us. There's so much to see. If Mami stopped she could find the complicated knots that will take years to undo. Nothing is in order.

"Marriage isn't easy," she says. "I love your father. But what held us together when I first met him isn't as strong. No se."

She continues. "I have no excuse for your father's actions but we've built a beautiful home for you and your brother, haven't we? You have the best of everything. You can't imagine what your life would have been if I had said no to your father. If I had stayed in Puerto Rico, taking care of your grandfather. The last of the sisters to marry. La fea. I was going to end up alone there. You don't know how my life would have ended. He took me away from there and look at where we are."

I study her. I examine the wrinkles around her eyes and the bony fingers. Even with her fallen face filled with sorrow, she's still prettier than my aunts. Mami told me kids used to tease her because she was darker than her sisters. A spectrum of skin color in one family, just like in mine. La fea. How is she the ugly one? That would make Junior, who looks just like her, ugly too. And me for being a part of her.

The story goes that Papi refused to work in the factory like he was expected to. Instead he moved to New York and took Mami with him. Mami transformed from this mousy little girl with pelo malo to this straightened-hair, eyeliner-wearing woman. New York meant freedom for her. My father may have picked her but it was Mami who made the final selection. So many desperate choices.

For once, I see more than a mother who craves order. I pick up the fallen rag and offer it to her.

"Here," I say.

With her face still concerned, she tucks one of my stray curls behind my ear.

"You understand, don't you?" she asks. Right then, she seems so young.

"Yes, Mami. Sure."

Outside, the slam of a car door is heard. Papi calls to her. Panic sets in. I'm not ready to face him. I can barely handle this moment with Mami. There's still the whole drug business with Junior I have to tell them about. How am I going to bring that up? I didn't even have a chance to share that nice little nugget with Elizabeth. Once I tell my parents, a whole new set of dramatics will be added to the mix. I can't deal with that right now.

"I can't see him," I tell her. "Please."

She nods and lets me go to my room.

I overhear my parents speaking in harsh whispers. Their voices rise and fall. I pull the shades down. Let them figure it out. Right now, I will try to sleep the morning off.

CHAPTER 25

A crashing sound wakes me from much too short of a nap. Dresser drawers are yanked open and slammed shut. Items are thrown to the floor. Before I can adjust to the noise, heavy footsteps stomp down the hallway toward my room.

"Did you go through my shit?" I notice Junior's saucer eyes. The warning signs that I once researched and wrote about for a school paper come back to me. Junior climbs onto my bed and drags me off it.

"Were you in my fucking room?" he says. "I'm going to kill you."

"Let go," I say. He pulls on my arms.

We've wrestled before, when we were young. Sometimes he would easily win. Other times I would win with a sucker punch or a mistaken kick to the groin. But this is no game.

Junior aims to drag me straight to his room. My kicks and screams alert everyone as he pulls me in.

"You fucking bitch. Why are you going through my shit?" He pins me down to the floor. "Tell me where it is before I wipe you all over this room."

"Are you crazy?" I yell back. "Let go."

"Where is it? I swear to God, if you don't tell me right now I'm going to punch the shit out of you!"

Somewhere during the night's commotion, I dropped the stash. It might be with the group of guys situated in front of the supermarket, giving them a seriously strong high. Or it could be by the community garden. I have no idea.

"Where the fuck is it?" Junior raises his hand ready to strike. I cower on the floor.

"Por Dios, Junior! Stop this!" Mami yells.

Papi grabs hold of Junior's shoulders and tosses him aside. With Junior's thin frame, it doesn't take much effort. Junior jumps up and rams Papi into the floor. Mami screams.

"Mind your business," Junior growls at him.

"Que carajo. Crees que es hombre." Papi gets up from the floor and pushes him against the wall. "Don't think I won't beat you because you're my son."

Part of me wants Junior to kick Papi's ass. To hit him for messing with those girls. I have hate for both of the men in my life but this anger isn't saved only for them. There's a little piece of it for Mami too as she tries to contain this drama.

Junior realizes he isn't battling little ol' me but both parents. He looks like a caged animal.

"She stole some money from me," he says. He tries to calm down.

"You better tell him," I say.

"This is bullshit," Junior says.

"Junior, what's going on?" Mami asks. "There must be a mistake." She's always the first to forgive him. Even when Papi told her that Junior was kicked out of school she blamed the university and the wrestling coach.

"Look, okay, it's not a big deal. Margot found some things in my room that don't belong to me," he says.

"There's a box filled with drugs and money," I say. "It's in the closet."

"Shut up, Margot. You don't know what you're talking about."

Papi storms to the closet. He tosses clothes everywhere. It doesn't take long for him to find the box. He dumps the contents on Junior's bed. Even as Junior swears innocence, the box spills forth the truth.

"You know how it is, how business works," Junior says. "C'mon, Papi, how you gonna believe Margot? She's just a stupid kid. She lied about Moises and about Oscar. Who do you think stole those cases of beer?"

"What is this, Junior?" Mami asks. I can see that her heart is breaking because there's no way she can defend this.

"No entiendo. Que haces con estas drogas?" She takes hold of his face and looks intensely at him. Junior pushes her hand away. He wants Papi.

"You always take Princesa's side. She can never do anything wrong, right?" he says. "I'm the fuck-up. I work like a slave, in return I get shit."

"You sat in my office with Oscar and you watched as I fired that man." Papi finally talks. "You knew the truth and you never said a word."

"Naw, Papi, c'mon," Junior says. His bony arms stay crossed in front of him. He shifts his weight from one leg to the next as if he can't decide which way to lean. "You know that's not true. I'm trying to do something here. It's business. This is temporary until I have enough cash for the bar. If you'd given me the money I wouldn't have to do this. As soon as I was established I would have put the money I borrowed from the supermarket back."

"You took me for a fool," Papi says. "I trusted you. Both of you."

Papi talks about trust when he's no expert. His eyes avoid mine as if he can read my mind. It's only a matter of time before Papi unleashes his wrath on Junior. The longer the silence, the more intense the atmosphere.

He picks up the money and places the bundles neatly back in the box. He grabs the little baggies filled with deadly rocks and puts them back too. Then Papi sits down by the edge of the bed with the box on his lap. He looks small. Old.

"Are things that bad between us?" Papi says.

He puts both hands on his face, and then he does the one thing I've never seen him do. Papi cries. The man who always knows what to say and when to say it, the man I believed could do no wrong, sobs.

Junior and I watch as Papi's whole body heaves with emotion so much that he shakes the bed. This terrifies me.

After a long moment, Mami walks over to Papi and places a hand on his shoulder. Then she trails her hand down his back.

"Ya, Victor. Cálmate," she says. He cries even more. She's never been so delicate with him. I'm rattled to witness this exchange and angry too. Let him cry. Let him suffer. But she won't. Mami lifts the box from his lap and tucks it under her arm.

"Come," she says. This time her voice is firm. "Vamos."

Mami cradles him with one arm like an injured child. Papi leans on her and she doesn't resist the burden. She holds him upright and walks him to their bedroom. Mami closes the door behind them.

Junior slides down to the floor. He curls his hands into fists and covers his eyes. Without making a sound, I leave him there.

CHAPTER 26

Papi tries again while I'm in the kitchen. The last time he started up a conversation with me I shot it down by dropping a glass full of water. Tiny pieces of shattered glass covered the tiled floor, reaching his brown dress shoes. It's only been a couple of days since the Sanchez family meltdown. There's no going back to that time when things were normal between us. The best I can do right now is to avoid him.

"Princesa." He calls to me as I exit the kitchen and leave my bowl of oatmeal untouched on the counter.

It's seven in the morning and this house is already unbearable. I go outside and get on my bike. Junior will probably be Papi's next target. There was another confrontation between them last night. Ultimatums made. The word "rehab" mentioned. Junior refuses to admit he has a problem. More screaming. More accusations. I don't want to stick around for a repeat performance.

The goal is to ride my bike to the nearest diner. Thankfully I have my laptop. I can stay here as long as I have to. From the diner's large windows, I'm able to see cars heading toward the city. It's Wednesday and I should be at the supermarket. I wonder what's going on there. I'm sure the whole place is aware of our dirty little secret. Apparently Mami convinced Oscar to take his job back. I can't believe he said yes. He should sue for wrongful termination or at least ask for a serious raise. He deserves it.

"Want some more?" the waitress asks. The diner is busy. I sit at the far end of the counter to be out of the way. The waitress recognized me. Elizabeth and I used to come here. We always shared the breakfast special: two eggs, bacon, and home fries.

This alone time gives me a lot to think about. Not everything is bad. There are glimpses of hope. Yesterday Mami dropped the divorce bomb on Papi. She said it loud, with serious conviction. Then again, it could have just been something she said in anger. I don't know. Either way, they need to work that out and keep it away from me.

I pull out my laptop and check e-mails. There are a couple from Serena. Questions about where I am and why I haven't responded to her texts. I'm not ready. Instead, I make a list.

GET REALLY REAL LIST
Elizabeth
Oscar
Nick
Moises
Serena/Camille

The names are not written in any particular order. I read in one of Mami's self-help books that if you want to do good you have to create the intention. Or maybe it was on *The View*. I can't be sure. I will try with this list.

After my third coffee refill, I hop back on the bike. In front of Elizabeth's house, her mom is working on the garden. I slow down.

"Hi, Mrs. Saunders." She wears a long Mexican dress and her toes are covered with dirt. Elizabeth's mom is a kindergarten teacher and there's always something arts and crafts about her.

"Good morning!" She has a gap between her two front teeth. Mami always wondered why she never got that fixed but I think it gives her character. "Elizabeth is out back."

"Thanks."

The door to the studio is wide open. A collection of pieces takes over one side of the room. The vibrant colors depict various city scenes. There are old men on souped-up

Schwinns. Another painting shows boys playing handball. Elizabeth sure knows how to capture summer.

I knock. Her expression is not her usual welcoming one but it's not evil either.

"Wow," I say. She is so talented.

"They're okay. They still need a lot of work," Elizabeth says. "What is it?"

"Oh, nothing," I say. "Want to go on a bike ride?"

It feels as if I'm asking her out on a date. I'm that nervous. I don't have a plan, just a responsibility to make amends for the way I've acted.

"I've got a lot of work to do," she says. "The block party is on Saturday and these still aren't done."

"Block party?"

"It's a fundraiser for the South Bronx Family Mission. Moises gave me a booth for free."

Moises. I swallow my jealousy.

"Are you selling them?" I ask.

"Yeah. We're going to give one away in a raffle."

We. She must mean her and Moises. I can't forget my intention. This is not about my feelings for him. This is about my friendship.

"Awesome," I say. "It's your first real public show. Congratulations."

We stand side by side for a moment and marvel at her

work. I have a lot of her old pieces but these are different. She has really improved. Why hadn't I noticed that before? "Well, you're busy. I'll see you."

I head toward the door. There's no need to push it. I'll let this happen naturally.

"Hey, wait," Elizabeth says. This is hard for her too. "I'm not going to make my deadline."

My heart kind of opens.

"You're not? Do you need help?" I don't care how eager I sound.

She nods.

"Yeah, of course," I say. "What do you need?"

"Paint. Materials."

"I can do that. Let's get a list together. I live for lists."

"Okay, let's make a list," she says.

I pull out my notebook, sit down on the futon, and wait for her to start. She rattles off names of items and once she finishes, I go off on my bike to buy the materials. It feels good to do something for someone. There's no time to rehash the past if I have to focus on the task in front of me.

When I come back I set the stuff on her coffee table.

"I have to head back home," I say. "I got everything on the list but you might have to go to the city for the real deals. That art store is so expensive."

Look at me, worried about money. Now I know life has turned upside down.

"If you want I can try to stop by later," I say. Junior isn't the only one on lockdown. I am too, for those stolen cases of beer. Everyone has to pay the price. My price includes a bunch of chores. Today is laundry day.

"You don't have to," Elizabeth says.

"No, I want to."

Elizabeth goes back to work and I get back on my bike.

CHAPTER 27

Elizabeth puts her brush down and walks away from the canvas. It's early Friday morning and I've been in her studio for two hours. I don't know how late she stayed up last night but she's in the same clothes from yesterday. And there's still so much to do.

"That painting looks similar to the other one," I say. "You know, the one of the park."

"You're right." She plops down to the floor and cradles her head. The block party is important to her. This is the first time she'll be displaying so many pieces. It's a huge endeavor.

"I'm never going to make it on time," she says. "I've still got two more to finish."

She might not see it but I can see the progress. The long hours in the studio have paid off. Elizabeth is almost done. She just needs to believe it.

"You have to offer people variety," I say. "How about looking at the park from another angle? Maybe from above like a bird."

She gets up and lets out a long sigh. Then she grabs a blank canvas and with charcoal starts to sketch another idea. It's pretty amazing to see how she can create a world with nothing but white space and black charcoal.

"Thanks," she says.

I tag the other paintings with titles and add the prices to an Excel sheet I created. Mami is letting me help Elizabeth but I still have a curfew. I want to stay in this studio and concentrate on her but I can't. I have my list. Today is as good a day as any to pick another name or two.

I text Serena and ask if she and Camille will be around in a half hour.

"I'm going to run a couple of errands. I'll be back." Elizabeth is so engrossed in her new work that she won't need me for a while.

I bike to a nearby park. Because it's early, the place is empty, with only a couple of joggers getting their health on. I'm not wearing any makeup. The T-shirt I borrowed from Elizabeth is splattered with paint. This is not how I should present myself but there's no time for a wardrobe change. Besides, it's exhausting to maintain a streamlined look every time I'm online with Serena and Camille. Not that I plan to abandon my love for fashion. There will be tweaks in my life but not end-of-the-world changes. I pull out a lipstick.

It's Serena and Camille's last weekend in the Hamptons. The parties will soon shift back to the city. Get-togethers to ease the Somerset students back into the grind. The old me would be so focused on scoring an invite. Even if I were interested I couldn't go to any parties, since I'm punished. The usual fall activities I do, like shopping for a new wardrobe, have been put on hold until further notice. Life right now is on full stop until Junior goes to rehab. That is, if he goes.

"Hi, Camille," I say. "Hi, Serena."

"Did you forget something?" Camille asks. She's angry. I've never ignored her texts or phone calls before. My actions must confuse her. "There are things we have to figure out, namely your next step with Nick and the party at—"

"I'm going through some serious stuff at home." I cut her off. "There are more important things happening right now in my life."

Will they ask how I feel? Do they even care? They both look so pretty but unattainable, like mannequins in the window of a department store.

"What's going on?" Serena asks. I know she cares. I can see it in her expression and how she leans into the screen. Still I hesitate.

"Nothing," I say. Typical. I revert right back to what they would expect from me. What will happen if I tell them the truth about my family? So what? If I can't be real with them I can't be real with anyone. I start over.

"I think my parents are getting a divorce and my brother . . ." I want to cover this up with an exaggerated story of some sort. Lies are so easy but I won't take that overused path. "My brother has a drug problem."

"Divorce!" Camille exclaims. "Is that all? My parents got a divorce. It happens to everyone. That's not a problem. It's just an annoyance."

Serena laughs but it's a nervous laugh. She can't help it.

"No, it's not an annoyance. My whole life is changing and . . . and . . ." I don't know if I can continue. This friend-ship will never grow if I keep my emotions in check. If I shoot down their chance to even respond, then this relation-ship is built on nothing.

"I'm scared."

There. I said it. There's a long silence.

"Does this mean you're not coming back to Somerset?" Camille asks. The only time she ever expresses interest is if the topic affects her in some way. But there's something in her tone that makes me think that maybe she cares.

"I'm coming back. I'm almost certain I am." The thought never crossed my mind that I wouldn't be returning. I guess I should take that into account too. Who knows what the future might bring?

Serena and Camille stay silent. It's hard to figure out what to say. I'm usually the one who'll do something reckless to cover that uncomfortable feeling. Not doing that feels weird.

"Well, this is a sucky way to end your vacation." Camille takes a sip from her water bottle.

"I wish my parents would get a divorce." Serena finally speaks up. "They argue twenty-four seven. If they got a divorce I'd get rooms in different places. It would be like having a vacation home and a real home. Double the closets, double the clothes. Right?"

If only things were that simple.

"Yeah, but what if they move to some place like Jersey or somewhere worse?" Camille says. "It wouldn't matter if you had two sets of clothes because you'd be in Jersey."

"Or the Bronx. Oh my god," Serena says. "Are you moving to the Bronx?"

"Technically, I live in the Bronx. Riverdale is in the Bronx." Time they learn the geography. "Anyway, the Bronx is not bad."

"You were the one who told us it's the worst place in the world!" Camille says.

"Yeah, you said it was a cesspool," Serena adds.

"Okay, okay. I did say that. I exaggerated. I was wrong. There are some great things here. Great people too."

Camille shrugs. It's not a dismissive shrug. I've seen those from her. It's more like acceptance.

"I was eight when my parents separated. He was screwing one of Mom's closest friends. She was practically family," Camille says. "Mom didn't sugarcoat a thing. She told me everything but I was too young. I kept expecting him to come back. Now I have to spend the holidays with that lady. I can't stand her."

This is the first time Camille has shared a side of her family life that isn't perfect. Her matter-of-fact tone tries to conserve her cool I-don't-care persona but I can see through it. Maybe there's something more to Camille underneath that high gloss. People sometimes can surprise you.

"Is your brother going to rehab?" Serena asks.

"I don't know," I say.

"Well, a lot of celebrities go to rehab. My mom designed this one house for this client and during the whole time he was detoxing but he didn't tell anyone," Camille says. "He just used the renovation as an excuse to get clean. Pretty smart, huh?"

"I don't think my family has that luxury," I say. Again there's an awkwardness that can't be ignored. It's strange not to fill up this moment with some extravagant tale to pretty up my reality.

"Well, I'll talk to you guys later," I say.

Serena and Camille can't believe I'm the one to end the phone call. Well, there's a first time for everything. It terrifies me to be this honest. I'm not used to it. I'm not sure whether our trio will continue or what form it might take.

I pedal back to the studio. Elizabeth's vision has come to life. It was only a matter of seeing things differently and taking a chance.

"What do you think?" Elizabeth asks.

"I think it's going to be great," I say, and I mean it too.

"I'll need help getting these to the block party," she says. "There's no way I'm going to be able to fit them all in my parents' car. Think your mom can drop us off?"

"I don't know. She barely lets me come here," I say. "What time do you have to be there?"

"Seven."

"Are you kidding? Who wakes up that early?"

I didn't know community activism started at that ungodly hour. Doesn't anyone believe in sleeping in on a Saturday? Injustice will still be there whether or not we're up at seven.

"You're up that early. Mom says she sees you riding your bike before dawn. Things are still bad at home, huh?"

"I'd rather eat scrambled eggs every morning at a diner by myself than see their faces."

"Then seven is going to be a breeze."

"I'll ask but I can't make any promises," I say.

"She'll say yes."

I go back to my Excel sheet. Moises will be there tomorrow. But I don't have time to obsess over that. I tag the rest of the paintings.

CHAPTER 28

A trio of old ladies set up long tables of food close to the entrance of the park. Burners are already lit. They're dressed in lunch lady outfits—aprons, hair tucked under a scarf, and plastic gloves, ready to serve. A guy begs them for a free sample. They shoo him away, slapping their towels at him like he's some pesky little boy.

Today's temperature will reach eighty degrees but it already feels like a hundred. We're going to bake. So not cute. These canvases are so big. Elizabeth and I wasted an hour figuring out how to pack them in the car. Plus, we didn't take into account the stands and how we intended to hang them up. Logistics. At one point, Elizabeth almost broke down after we realized there was no room for her in the car. A couple of the pieces had to stay.

"Just up ahead," Elizabeth says.

Although I moaned when I got the wake-up call, the drive to the park was fun. Elizabeth told me about the crazy characters at the museum. I told her about my own supermarket dustups, minus any mention of Jasmine or Moises. Mami was nice enough to let us catch up. She even smiled at our stories. I promised to call her an hour before the party ended so that she can pick us up.

There's no stopping the anxiety that surges inside and will not die down no matter how many funny stories we exchange. Luckily, Moises is not the first person we see.

"Oh my god. You killed it, sister. Killed it!" Paloma screams from across the park as we hang the first canvas. "Muchacha. You are so gifted."

I'm proud too. The pieces are amazing now that they're no longer in the studio but out in the open.

"So good to see you," Paloma says to me. "That dance floor is ours."

There isn't an actual dance floor, just a concrete space that faces the circular stage where the deejay is set up. Music already blares.

"It's good to see you too," I say.

When Paloma comes in for a hug, I don't shy away.

She sets up a table next to ours. She's selling jewelry and will donate some of her funds to the community center. Her jewelry is big and bold, just what I expect from her. One necklace stands out. A crude leather strand holds a large silver charm. The charm is a square box and inscribed in the tiniest of letters is the following:

Don't let the hand you hold
Hold you down.
—JdB

"What does 'JdB' stand for?" I ask.

"Julia de Burgos, of course," Paloma says. "The Puerto Rican Goddess."

Julia de Burgos, the poet.

"How much do you want for it?"

"Because it's going to you, give me what you can afford."

I look in my purse. There's not much money to be had these days. But the necklace is so pretty. I don't want to insult Paloma with a few measly dollars. She deserves more. Before, I wouldn't even think twice about spending cash for what I wanted. I could always count on Papi to pick up the tab. But that life is sort of dead now. I have to figure my own financial way. I set the necklace back down.

"Let's barter," Paloma says.

But what do I have to offer? I'm not an artist. I don't make jewelry or play an instrument. My expensive lockets have been confiscated as payback for the stolen beers. I have nothing to give. I'm broke.

"I don't have anything."

"Well. It's an expensive piece," she says. "Give me what cash you have now, but when you're back at school, direct your friends right to my Etsy shop. Let them know where you got it."

"I know exactly who would love this. The A La Mode Club," I say. "It's a fashion club. They have a style blog and everything. They would die for this."

The student who runs the fashion club is Karen. We sat next to each other in math class last year. Karen has always been nice to me. Not super friendly but then again, I wasn't looking to make a new friend since my efforts were concentrated on Serena and Camille.

"They invite designers and businesspeople to speak to the members," I say. "They take it very seriously. Maybe you can come and talk to them about your designs and then sell them afterwards."

"Margot knows about publicity," Elizabeth says.

I'm excited about this. This can totally be my thing come fall. I can find ways to promote Paloma's jewelry and maybe Elizabeth's art, if she'll let me.

"Moises, I need more juice here."

The deejay yells out for more electricity. My heart drops a bit. A couple of deep breaths and I look over to Elizabeth. She's so wrapped up in making sure everything looks good that nothing is breaking her out of it. When I see Moises walk toward us I do the lame thing and hide behind a canvas.

"You guys need anything?" Moises pops his head into the tent. "Oh, hey."

He didn't expect to see me.

"Hey." My throat goes dry. I wait for him to go over to Elizabeth and give her a kiss or hug, an appropriate greeting for a new couple, but he doesn't. Sure, Elizabeth hasn't brought him up much other than mentioning the festival but I figured that's just evidence that she's hiding their relationship from me.

"We can use some more rope," I say. "Do you have any?"

Elizabeth agrees.

"One sec." Moises goes off and I'm relieved that I didn't fall flat on my face. He soon comes back with the rope, then leaves again as someone else calls out for help. Elizabeth barely looks at him.

One of the easels topples over. I run to help Elizabeth before the whole thing crashes to the ground. Strange how she didn't give Moises the time of day. She doesn't have to pretend on my account. I can handle their coupling.

"You don't have to play it safe for me," I say.

Elizabeth looks confused.

"You and Moises," I say.

She sets the canvas down. "What are you talking about?"

"Nothing. I mean, you guys are so, um, cold to each other. You don't have to be. I'm okay with it."

"Okay with what?"

She really wants me to spell it out.

"Going out. You and Moises seeing each other. I'm fine with it."

"Hahaha." She snorts. "Moises? Me and Moises?"

Even Paloma joins in on the laughter.

"I'm not seeing Moises," Elizabeth says. "Hahaha!"

"I just thought since you guys spend so much time . . ."

"Oh, Margot. You can be so dumb. We're friends. Besides, he's not my type. I like artists. You know that."

"I did. I mean I used to. I don't know. I'll shut up now," I mumble. This makes them both giggle even more.

The mind is such a tricky thing. I basically created a whole relationship based on jealousy. Not sure when I'll ever let that trait go and learn to trust those around me. This won't happen overnight. It will take practice.

The deejay turns down the music. Moises takes to the microphone and is joined by a few important-looking men and one frail grandma type.

"Thank you for coming out to the Stop the Orion Community Block Party. This is going to be a full day. Bella will be doing some arts and crafts activities over there for the kids. Raise your hand, Bella! And definitely check out Elizabeth's paintings. We will be raffling one off to a lucky winner. A dollar a ticket. All funds go to the community."

"And what if I don't win?" jokes a young mother who

holds a baby girl. "I'm serious. Dollar can't buy much but I need my money. What can you give me in return, boo?"

Poised as he is, Moises is caught off guard and doesn't have a quick comeback. This is his thing and yet there he is onstage at a total loss.

"Honey, you're holding the mike. I want to win something. What can you do for me?" she says, high-fiving her friend. The crowd enjoys seeing Moises squirm. I do too.

Moises laughs. He's nervous.

"Don't worry, baby." She lets up after a few more jabs. "I'll let you do your thing."

"Thank you," he says, and pulls out a bandana to wipe his forehead. "DJ Forty is going to do his thing. But first, here's someone I want you to meet. This is Doña Petra. She's been living at the Eagle Avenue building, the same building Carrillo Estates wants to tear down for some overpriced condos."

Doña Petra isn't shy at all. She grabs hold of the microphone and yells into it. The noise wakes everyone up. Moises whispers to her and she starts again.

"I live here. Yo vivo aquí," Doña Petra says. "Ustedes me conocen. And I say it too in English, porque sí. This is my home and I don't want to live anywhere else."

Doña Petra talks with such passion. Everyone feels the energy. Even I feel it. She has a right to her home. We all do.

"Help me stay here with you," she says. "Mi familia."

"That's right!" says Paloma. "We got your back, Doña!"

"You better believe it!" I yell. Elizabeth and Paloma both turn to me.

"Look at Margot," Paloma says. "Who knew she was so Boogie Down?"

"Maybe I am," I say.

I don't see Moises for the rest of the event. He's way too busy, which is fine. I'm busy too, dancing with Paloma.

CHAPTER 29

The piragüero greets me with a "Buenos días." He's by the train station, in the line of fire. Although it's eight in the morning, way too early for a frozen crushed ice treat, I pay for one anyway. The sugary-sweet cherry-flavored ice tastes so good.

When I told Mami I wanted to come in to work she couldn't understand why. School starts this Wednesday and technically I completed my ten weeks of work. But I told her I had a few things to finish. There are apologies that need to be made.

I walk into the supermarket as Oscar goes over the agenda for the month, which includes back-to-school specials. I stand in the back with the stock boys. Everyone whispers around me. My appearance here is the bochinche of the day. I'm sure they've analyzed what went down with my family and who can blame them? It's the story of the century and it's got everything in it—sex, drugs, and betrayal. No need to watch any soaps. Just follow the Sanchez & Sons daily drama.

"The candy stands have to be replenished and placed in front of the cashiers," Oscar says. He sits comfortably atop the conveyor belt, the spot Papi usually occupies. Running the meeting is simple for Oscar. He knows what to do.

Papi is at the Kingsbridge location. The rumor about the store being shut down is true. Roughly fifty people are about to lose their jobs. It's terrible. The new shopping complex is already holding cattle-call interviews for the new supermarket. The complex will also house a Target and a BJ's Wholesale Club. The neighborhood is changing and there's a sense that everything has to be buckled down to keep people from losing their stake. My guess is that my family will hold on to the original Sanchez & Sons supermarket for as long as they can. I try my best not to jump to the future. The what-ifs can keep a person frozen, keep them from doing anything. Instead, I take baby steps. For example, dishes were not thrown at Papi's feet this week. Progress.

After the meeting concludes, Rosa settles in at the first register, the register that belongs to Jasmine. Rosa digs into her purse and pulls out a small statue of Jesus on the cross. Before securing the statue on a corner visible to each customer, she kisses it and crosses herself.

Another reason why I came. I was assured that Jasmine wouldn't be here. They've given her a sort of medical leave. She has high blood pressure and the stress is too much for the pregnancy. Jasmine is keeping the baby. I get so angry thinking about it. Elizabeth told me it's Jasmine's decision and I should try not to judge her for it. Of course I'm going to judge her. Her choice is causing so much destruction. Then again, my parents haven't been living that marital bliss life for some time. My fluctuating emotions make me dizzy.

I walk upstairs to the office. Oscar stands over the desk.

"Do you have a moment?" I ask.

"Sí," he says.

"I'm sorry for the lies I told and the stealing," I say. "I'm sorry for the pain I caused you and your family."

Oscar's expression is serious. There are no jolly grins this time around.

"I also have this to give you." I hand him a sealed envelope. "It's from Junior."

It took Mami everything to convince Junior that it was time for him to get help. They found a rehab somewhere upstate.

"I fucked up, Margot," Junior said the night before he left for Carmel. No truer words have been uttered. He looked so dejected, like he'd been on a treadmill going nowhere for hours.

"I'm gonna make things right," he said. "Watch. I'm

going to change. I'm going to stop hanging with them bums."

A thought crossed my mind, something I'd been wanting to ask him.

"What was it about Moises that made you hate him so much?"

"I didn't hate him. Look, I don't want any guy talking to my sister," Junior said. Then he shook his head. "After I got kicked off the team, his brother helped me deal with it. I didn't need Moises telling you that."

I didn't press him for more details. I understood what he meant. Secrets can cause more pain than facing the truth head-on. I continued to help him pack, and underneath a pile of clothes on the floor I spotted a familiar light blue color. With my toe, I nudged away the pile and unearthed the lost Tiffany box.

"There it is." I reached down and traced the edges of the empty box with my finger. "It was pretty."

"Yeah, it was," he said. "I'll buy you another one."

"No, I don't need one."

He stopped packing. "You don't think I can do it?" He held the sides of his suitcase as if he were thinking about jumping in.

"No, that's not it." I pushed his hand away so that I could fold another shirt. "I'm too old for charm necklaces. Now, if you want to buy me some diamond earrings . . ."

"Aw, I see how you are," he said.

Before he left, he handed me the envelope and asked me to give it to Oscar. A written apology for now. It's a start. We both have to do more.

"You know, Oscar, I bet your wife needs a little break. I can babysit whenever you want," I say. "During the weekends."

"Oh no. Con eso muchachos? Estás loca. They will break you into two. Did I tell you what I caught them doing the other day?" he asks. There's a glint in his eyes. "They took my cell phone and started calling long distance, looking for their abuela. No, those two are a handful."

Out of habit, he pulls out the picture in his wallet and shows it to me. I act as if it's my first time seeing it. The lie is worth it just to see his happiness.

"I can handle the boys," I say. "Please let me do this. Let's figure out a day."

He eventually agrees. On my phone I pull up the website I created for the supermarket using a simple template. The site isn't live yet so it's still pretty rough. It's going to take some time to build an audience but I have some ideas. We talk about promoting the sales of the week and profiling the workers. I suggest Roberto because I can already envision the side-eye picture.

Downstairs, Dominic stocks the cans of tomato sauce. I walk over to him and open the box next to him. I left my usual fashion uniform home. It's easier to work in jeans.

287

"How's your girlfriend?" I ask.

"Chilling," he says. "This is the longest I've ever been with one girl. She might be the one."

"Really?" He hands over the price gun. I'm faster when it comes to pricing. "Are you talking wedding?"

"Naw, you crazy," he says. "I'm talking about going all the way."

I shake my head at him, and then notice when he glances over to the front of the supermarket. I wonder if he is as nervous as I am about Jasmine popping up unannounced.

It's impossible to banish Jasmine from my thoughts. I tried everything. Hating her with such passion that I made myself sick. Then shame replaced the anger and then went back to anger. Elizabeth thought I was crazy to come back here knowing Jasmine might be around. This is Jasmine's neighborhood but I don't want to live my life afraid of crossing the street. This isn't where I live but it's where my family works. This place will always be a part of me.

How do I feel about a possible half sister or half brother in the family? I can't even begin to wrap my head around it. It's going to take a lot of time and probably a lot of therapy. Mami is looking into someone for me to talk to and I'm okay with that.

"You heard the latest by MiT?" Dominic asks. Before I answer him, he raps the song to me. His hair is even more shellacked today.

"It's okay," I say.

"Damn, Princesa, you're hard to please," he says.

We soon fall into a rhythm. He hands me a can. I price it and place it on the shelf. He opens another box and we start again. Dominic hums the song and soon the song seeps in and I hum along.

CHAPTER 30

The plan was always to reach out to him. I made that decision even before I saw him at the block party. Moises *is* on my Get Really Real List so it was just a matter of time. When and where. Still, sending the text wasn't easy. I compiled a list of possible asks. Number three ultimately won out: Are you available to meet me for lunch? I opted for formality instead of the casual number five: Hey, you hungry? which might have read like it came from some insane girl.

It took Moises exactly thirty-two minutes to respond to my text. Thirty-two excruciatingly long minutes. He agreed to meet me at his favorite bench. The walk here was filled with anxiety and it has increased tenfold now that I see him sitting there waiting for me.

"I got you a Cuban sandwich," I say, and hand him the

brown paper bag. Moises peeks in and nods approval.

"Thanks," he says. I sit next to him and try to let go of some of my nervousness. He wears a green shirt with an image of an old album cover titled *The Fania All-Stars* and his worn jeans.

"So, I heard what went down," he says. "How's your brother doing?"

"He's handling it. Rehab is hard but he's trying. My family is going through some serious changes," I say. "Anyway, thanks for answering my text and for meeting me."

Moises nods his head.

"Yeah, I feel you about changes," he says. "It looks like the city will probably give Carrillo Estates the green light for the condos." He juts his chin out to where the Royal Orion will be built.

"Oh, I'm so sorry," I say. I thought for sure Moises and the Family Mission had a strong chance of beating Carrillo Estates. "That's awful."

"Yeah, it's a tough fight but it will be a long process. They still have a bunch of hurdles to overcome. This is just the beginning. We'll have to step up our game or the families will be the real victims."

We let that sink in while we eat our sandwiches.

"I start Somerset Prep on Wednesday," I say, sounding a little glum. "I guess summer is officially over."

Mami has planned a mother-daughter weekend getaway

in Connecticut. Just the two of us. She said something about wanting to check out the antique shops. Papi is staying at his cousin's in Yonkers. Without the drama of Junior, the house is super quiet. I don't know what's going to happen to my parents. Divorce? Probably. Jasmine being pregnant can't possibly be a good thing for a marriage. There are times when Mami seems strong and determined. Other times when she doesn't even bother concealing her tears from me. We're each trying to deal with the situation differently and it's in no way perfect.

"So, I thought you didn't want to have anything to do with me," Moises says. "What's up?"

Although he tries to sound cold he's not directly looking at me. Instead, he concentrates on the ground. And because I'm as nervous as he is, I keep focused on my sandwich.

"Nothing. I was just wondering . . . What I mean is . . ." I'm rambling. I've got to pull myself together. This is something I want to do.

"I wanted to apologize for the way I treated you that night in the Hamptons. For everything. I was mean and you didn't deserve it, not when you were just trying to help me," I say. "Even with what happened between us, I still want to be friends. That is, if you want to."

He goes silent and it takes everything in me not to run away. It's not easy being real. This new path is unfamiliar. Moises agreed to lunch but he doesn't owe me a friendship or anything else for that matter. I rub the etched words on the new necklace I got from Paloma and wait.

"What about your boy Nick?" he asks. "Your fancy school friends. What about them?"

"There are no boys. There's only me," I say. "That's it. Just me."

Eventually I face him. We smile. Two goofy grins.

We sit there and watch the kids play.

ACKNOWLEDGMENTS

First I must thank editor Zareen Jaffery, Mekisha Telfer, and the rest of the Simon & Schuster staff for not only making my dream come true but for making this such a warm and effortless first publishing experience. A heartfelt thanks must go to my amazing agent, Eddie Schneider of JABberwocky Literary Agency, for pulling my novel from the slush pile. It does happen. I will forever be grateful.

To my writer's group (Elizabeth, Hilary, Cindy, Jason, Josh, and Mary), thank you for being such early champions of my work. I am indebted to author and generous instructor Al Watt for instilling the belief that I could actually write a novel. I also owe a lot to PEN Center USA for awarding me a 2013 Emerging Voices Fellowship and for connecting me with my kind mentor, children's author Cecil Castellucci. I am grateful to the Elizabeth George Foundation, whose generous grant allowed me the time and resources to complete this novel.

Thanks goes to Jean Ho for always being there. And a big love goes to Kima Jones of Jack Jones Literary Arts for talking me out of many meltdowns.

Love is sent to my family living in the Bronx, Puerto Rico, and beyond. To my beautiful nieces, Taina and Brianne, for always sharing my passion for young adult books. Big hugs are due to Melody, Tonalli, Antonio, and Ariana. I am also forever indebted to the collective energy, humor, and belief of my talented siblings, Annabel, Hector, Edgardo, and Osvaldo, and my parents, Hector and Ana. Our shared memories and love for the Bronx helped shape this novel.

My two beautiful daughters, Isabelle and Sophia Colette, are my constant inspirations. I love you both. And lastly, no amount of words can express how much I owe my husband, David. Thank you for everything.

DISCOVER NEW YA READS

READ BOOKS FOR FREE

WIN NEW & UPCOMING RELEASES

RIVETED

YA FICTION **IS OUR ADDICTION**

JOIN THE COMMUNITY

DISCUSS WITH THE COMMUNITY

WRITE FOR THE COMMUNITY

CONNECT WITH US ON RIVETEDLIT.COM

AND @RIVETEDLIT

From

Morgan Matson,

the bestselling author of *Since You've Been Gone*, comes a
feel-good story of friendship, finding yourself, and all the joys in
life that happen while you're busy making other plans.

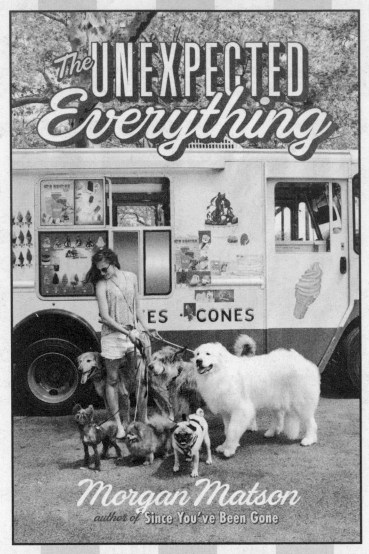

PRINT AND EBOOK EDITIONS AVAILABLE
From SIMON & SCHUSTER BFYR
simonandschuster.com/teen